Other People's Fun

Also by Harriet Lane

Her
Alys, Always

Other People's Fun

HARRIET LANE

Little, Brown and Company
New York Boston London

Copyright © 2025 by Harriet Lane

Hachette Book Group supports the right to free expression and the value of copyright. The purpose of copyright is to encourage writers and artists to produce the creative works that enrich our culture.

The scanning, uploading, and distribution of this book without permission is a theft of the author's intellectual property. If you would like permission to use material from the book (other than for review purposes), please contact permissions@hbgusa.com. Thank you for your support of the author's rights.

Little, Brown and Company
Hachette Book Group
1290 Avenue of the Americas, New York, NY 10104
littlebrown.com

First North American Edition: November 2025
Originally published in the United Kingdom by Weidenfeld & Nicolson: October 2025

Little, Brown and Company is a division of Hachette Book Group, Inc. The Little, Brown name and logo are trademarks of Hachette Book Group, Inc.

The publisher is not responsible for websites (or their content) that are not owned by the publisher.

The Hachette Speakers Bureau provides a wide range of authors for speaking events. To find out more, go to hachettespeakersbureau.com or email hachettespeakers@hbgusa.com.

Little, Brown and Company books may be purchased in bulk for business, educational, or promotional use. For information, please contact your local bookseller or the Hachette Book Group Special Markets Department at special.markets@hbgusa.com.

ISBN 9780316369947
Library of Congress Control Number: 2025942060

Printing 1, 2025

LSC-C

Printed in the United States of America

For Barnaby

I look. I can't stop looking. That's the deal, isn't it? We all know that's how it works. If someone wants to be seen – and oh, how they want to be seen – then someone has to watch. The pageant needs its audience, and that's where I come in. Rapt, attentive, free to draw my own conclusions. I wonder if they ever think about that.

I wonder if they understand they are nothing without me.

We are nearly there. Jean turns right at the fingerpost and follows the road through the village, and though some of it is new – the antique shop, the deli with its humbug awning – most of it is horribly, shamingly familiar, a reminder that I'll never escape this place, no matter what I tell myself. War memorial, flint church, the half-timbered pub we never went to because it was popular with staff, and then Miss Balfour's redbrick villa, and the bursar's house, and somehow I miss the drive leading to the ugly bungalow where I occasionally babysat for the Waxham children. The foaming hedgerows rise up and fall away, streaming behind us like a wake, an illusion that makes me feel slightly seasick. Jean is telling me about pulling a muscle during a recent walking holiday in the Abruzzo, describing in some detail her physio routine of stretches and rotations.

I nod and murmur and press my palms on my skirt, and there's the blue sign and the gate dragged open to the verge. Jean taps the indicator. 'Here we are,' she says, hauling at the wheel. 'Goodness – what on earth is *that*?'

'It's the new art department,' I say, humiliated that I know this, because really, I shouldn't study the old pupils'

Bulletin, which is essentially a termly begging letter: I have better things to do with my time, and I certainly have better things to do with my money. 'I think it won a RIBA award.'

A boy in a Ramones T-shirt, the sort of vintage shirt also popular in our day, steps out of the shade of the Humanities Building and comes towards the car. His mouth moves. Amazing teeth. I roll down my window: 'We're here for the—'

'Keep going – loads more space by the music school, if you need it, but you should be fine,' he says, and his beautiful eyes are full of pity.

Jean noses the car into the shade of an oak and we sit there for a moment, gazing at the Jacob sheep on the other side of the fence. An old Nissan crawls into the space next to us. I don't recognise the occupants. Two elderly women – well, older than us, at any rate. Jean starts digging around in her bag. 'Oh, you will think I'm terribly rude – I've been gabbling away,' she says, applying ChapStick. 'So much to catch up on. How is Elizabeth? And Robert? Everyone well?'

'Elizabeth is fine. Yes, Robin, he's fine too.' Then, quite hesitantly, because in her birthday cards and January phone calls she has never mentioned a partner, I say, 'And you, is there...?'

'There is not,' she says, without rancour or discomfort, and reaches for the door handle. We get out and fuss around with litter and bags, and finally we can't put it off any longer so we join the thin procession snaking past the Wye Building over the Meadow towards the New Hall, which is, of course, quite old. The sun has come out, filling the grass and the turning leaves with a golden light, a light I remember from those other Septembers, and the groups of boarders lazing in the Meadow are illuminated too: their hair and bare legs, their wrists strung with twine bracelets, which remind me of the Donne poem I surely encountered here. They lean on each other, chatting, oblivious to us. Carrying over some distance, there's the crack and whoop of a six.

A charming path has been mown through the long grass, and we follow it. Jean continues to express thoughts as they occur, much as she did on the short drive from the station. I don't know her well enough to be sure if this is nerves or her default setting, but her voice is loud and clear. Some girls glance in our direction and then carefully turn away, as if they daren't look at us or each other, though I can't be sure if this is out of amusement, or horror, or a sort of delicacy. We must seem sad wraiths to them, I suppose: awkward visitors from the past, claiming some kind of ungainly kinship; or perhaps emissaries from a dread future from which all the things that make life worthwhile – youth, fun, possibility – have been stripped away. No wonder they avert their eyes.

Everything is of interest to Jean: the planting scheme around the library steps, the monstrous science extension, the renovation of the clock tower. Something seems to be suspended from the clock tower: a length of shiny pink material, which twists a little, catching the breeze. Jean reminds me that the night before our final Founders' Day a dressmaker's dummy was stolen from the textile studio, zipped into Mr Trickett's red anorak, and winched up there on a noose.

'Isn't that Verity Spackman?' Jean says, and I have a momentary flash of a forceful girl in a brown kilt, someone I would hide from after history, for fear of getting stuck with her for lunch. Thanks to the *Bulletin* and social media, I know Verity Spackman is now something significant at Google, a runner of half-marathons, a cold-water swimmer and the mother of three high-achievers. 'And look, look, there's Dribbler!'

Dribbler has turned into a mild-looking person in a button-down shirt and hiking trainers, treading a cigarette butt into the cobbles. What was Dribbler's real name? Duncan? Martin? Martin Duncan? I do remember that Dribbler liked heavy metal and was known to keep an airgun hidden in his study in the science block. From time to time he would crack the window and take aim at the little boys making their way to games, so they cried out and raced for cover, clapping hands to their arms or thighs. Dribbler became Dribbler after the Tybalt–Mercutio fight scene got out of hand in Miss Capstick's drama workshop. I remember the tittering as he lurched to his feet and staggered around, a shoelace of drool swinging from his jaw as he mumbled for Mummy. They – we – never forgot that Mummy.

We step off the Meadow into the small crowd outside the New Hall. Jean darts ahead, waving, seizing people and kissing them, as if this is terrific fun, such a lark, while I trail behind, a smile stuck to my teeth. We've all changed, lost hair or put on weight, gained crows' feet and what we believe to be stylish eyewear, and yet even in this quick instant I recognise the tics and mannerisms of those long-lost adolescents, last seen a lifetime ago, before the realities of life obliterated us or showed us who we really were. Someone in an olive moleskin jacket moves aside to let us pass. His back is turned but I know those shoulders, that neck, those ears. It comes at me with sudden force, a sentimental assault, and just for a moment every sensible thought is knocked out of me. Just for a moment I am overwhelmed, as I always was; overwhelmed by fear or longing, a combination of both.

Absurd. Of course, I am now far older than he was then. I inch past, careful not to touch him, focusing on Jean, who has now reached the steps. A yawning girl is handing out printed sheets. There's a photograph of Mr Power (we called him Talc, because his first name was Malcolm) on the front: ruddy and jovial, slightly sweaty, as if recently returned from one of his favourite activities – bowling an over, perhaps, or hunting down smokers in the Witch Wood.

The New Hall is already quite full, and I maintain a lively and amused expression as we enter it, though I'm now in the grip of another powerful nostalgia, an echo of the suspense that always came when you went in for Drones, when you prayed that someone had saved you a seat, because if they hadn't you'd have to walk to the front, searching for a space, and people might start calling out remarks about your weird hair, or the fact that no one ever fancied you.

The benches still fill up from the rear but there is no cat-calling today, just a few smiles, a nod or two, some civilised finger-waving. We sidle along a pew beneath one of the stained-glass windows and, when seated, I study the handout, waiting for the absurd adolescent percussion to slow a little. *Breathe*, I remind myself. *Breathe. This is crazy.*

I didn't really get much of a look at him and yet somehow he made an impression: the same, yet different, like the rest of us. He was only ten years older than us, in his late twenties back then. Early thirties at the most. Retirement now in his sights.

Sitting here, bathed in the light of the stained glass – an

eerie light, long-forgotten and yet immediately familiar – time seems to bunch and wrinkle, as if drawn together by a clumsy seamstress, and it's thrilling, and also a torment, to find myself in proximity to that faraway self and all her violent desires.

The noise in the New Hall dies away as Mrs Power is shown to her seat, and then the newish head, a woman in a magenta shirt-dress and statement necklace, rises and welcomes us all, reminding us of the Howard ethos, the enduring values of endeavour and fellowship, and of Malcolm Power's tireless commitment to those principles in the classroom and on the playing field; and how, well into his nineties, he remained an enthusiastically forthright presence both on the touchline and in governors' meetings. Amusement ripples through the room.

A tenor, a newish leaver, sings 'Silent Noon'. A girl reads some Edward Thomas. In an affectionate tribute, the current head of history describes being interviewed for a junior post twenty years ago, on an afternoon when Talc couldn't quite bring himself to switch off *Test Match Special*. A Power granddaughter plays the Allegro from Bach's Sonata in E Minor on the flute. An Old Boy in a senior role at the *Financial Times* describes Talc getting so worked up about the Ashes that after an away match he piloted the school minibus into a ditch.

Shifting on the hard benches, we think about the chasm between then and now, all the things the chasm contains.

Now the chamber choir shuffles forward to sing us out. Yes, there he is, materialising over the heads in front of me, taking up position with his back – just the faintest glimmer of a bald patch – to the audience. Lifting his hands, he waits, index fingers raised; and it seems to me he occupies the space between this pair of inverted commas as if he is indeed the point, the whole point. He is entirely at ease in the charged air, as he always was; and though I cannot see it, I remember his expression – eyebrows raised, teeth bared – as he prepared to bring us in.

In the hush, I feel the pressure of the old Drones nightmare, as forceful and dangerous as steam. For a moment it seems I may be swept away by the nightmare's recurring protocol, familiar for many decades: I will get to my feet, here in the New Hall, here in this pink and green light, and I will open my mouth and speak into the silence, and everyone will turn to look at me. And when this happens I will realise that I am not wearing any clothes, and a shudder of astonishment and revulsion and glee will spill through the room. And then the laughter.

The music starts. It's an acapella version of 'Blackbird'. The sound soars towards the rafters, clear and true. There's the horrifying smart of tears. Jean leans close and whispers, 'Look – *Waxham*.'

I blink and make a little gesture – *is it?* – while the teenagers sing about suffering and patience and release.

* * *

It's important to feign ignorance. People would be uncomfortable if I seemed too familiar with the details of their lives, so I stand in the buttery, the air humid with the exhalations of tea urns, and pretend I know nothing. 'Really?' I say, and 'Congratulations!' and 'You *have* been busy!' although, thanks to social media and the *Bulletin*, I am up to speed on most of it: the careers, the marriages and children, even the dogs and holidays and kitchen extensions, and (this is just starting to happen where the men are concerned) the next round of weddings and babies. On a day like this, I keep my powder dry.

It's no hardship. I am used to asking the questions. Curiosity is sanctuary, camouflage, an open sesame. You ask, and their cheeks flush with the excitement and pleasure of talking about themselves. Even if you already know the answers, or have little interest in them, questions unlock other useful things: good will, breathing space, possibly a little power.

Standing here – burning, ludicrously, with the knowledge that Waxham is over there, a scone's throw away, with his Tattersall shirt and impressively rumpled hair – I am aware that most people can't immediately place me. Everyone remembers Jean (who was always a singular character in our year, much mocked for her old-lady name and her unselfconscious diligence in the library) but they turn to me with a blank polite expression.

I learned I was being sent to Howard on the eve of the autumn term. My father was dispatched to the Toronto office at very short notice, and boarding fees were part of the package, so without warning I was removed from my old life (my best friend Nell, a bedroom to myself, a sense of being cared for) and dropped into strange territory where everyone but me knew the rules. It felt as if I never quite overcame that disadvantage.

Howard had two big points in its favour: proximity to the airport, and a spare place. As term started, it became apparent I was one of only a handful of new arrivals. The school was climbing out of one of its sporadic scandals (the expulsion of several sixth formers who'd been supplying the pupil body with the help of a dealer in Westbourne Grove), an episode that was of interest to the red-tops because minor royals with artistic leanings sent their children there, and also rock stars who turned up to Founders' Day in helicopters and fur coats. (Later, I understood that the parents who stuck with Howard at this moment probably did so because they were simply too busy with their own crazy shit. Or perhaps, like my parents, they didn't read the tabloids.)

My Howard career was not particularly distinguished. My ambition, socially, was to fly under the radar, and clearly I did a good job because Dribbler confuses me with Clare Snape, and Alexia Freemantle, with whom I shared a study, assumes we were in different years. But Verity Spackman spots me across the room and starts to zig-zag through the crowd, semaphoring energetically. I'll admit I'm a little flattered. 'Ruth! I always wondered what happened to you,' she says, and I remember all the small easy betrayals, the times I hid in the drying room rather than walk down to Crowfield with her on Saturday afternoon, or shuffled my chair sideways so there was no space for her to squeeze in beside me at breakfast. She's a handsome woman now. Great hair, skilful make-up, a structured jacket that might well be vintage Westwood. Yes, I say, I am on Facebook, but I am not very good at it.

We begin on common ground: with Talc, who inspired Verity to read history (Cambridge – she can't resist reminding me, as a matter of urgency).

I say I wasn't planning to come today but Jean Pugh got in touch, quite out of the blue, and I thought: why not? So kind of her to pick me up from the station. I mention I feel a bit of a fraud being here; history wasn't my strong suit and I found Talc rather terrifying. 'Oh, that's right, you did modern languages,' Verity says, startling me by remembering. Now we must summarise our professional achievements over the last few decades. Necessarily broad-brush. I put a positive spin on mine and, courteously, she downplays hers. As I over-egg the literary aspect, I experience a queasy shame, but of course she would glaze over if I started talking about the bread-and-butter stuff, the legal and marketing translations that pay the bills.

There's a little awkward pause as we wonder whether to get more personal and it seems we decide against, because Verity remarks on how warm it is and asks if I remember the blistering day after exams when Dribbler's friends threw him into the Humanities fishpond and he lolled there in the shallows, basking among the bullrushes, until Mr Waxham made him climb out.

'Rather unnerving to see Waxham again,' Verity says, lowering her voice. 'Can't believe he's still here!'

'Who? Oh, yes!' I say, and then I feel the need to add, 'I never really saw the point.'

'Then you were the only one,' she says, waving away fruitcake. Now she looks back on it, she thinks it was a group hysteria, like *The Crucible* – wasn't that one of our set texts? All the boys were so hopeless, and then Waxham arrived, and suddenly we were all joining the choir or taking up the clarinet. 'He got off on all the attention, and who can blame him? Stuck down a lane in the middle of nowhere, and here's this ready-made fan club. And of course, though we couldn't see it ourselves at the time, we were all absolutely *gorgeous*. He must have felt like Simon Le Bon.'

I smile and nod, perhaps a little embarrassed for her. It occurs to me that Waxham is the only thing we all have in common.

OTHER PEOPLE'S FUN

Someone jostles past, murmuring apologies as tea slops into my saucer. Verity bends close again, caught up in the old melodrama. God help her, *he's still kind of hot.* Years of conditioning at an impressionable age, well, you can't just shake it off. 'You must remember the last Founders' Day concert when Clare Snape bodged her cello solo and Sookie Utley fainted halfway through *Carmina Burana*, and Waxham carried her out, and the look on her face ... it was like that scene in *An Officer and a Gentleman*. Sookie's here, actually. Have you spoken to her?'

'Sookie? No.' I never spoke to her then; I won't start now. A series of Instagram images come to mind: dim sum in Kowloon; infinity pools crammed with fruit inflatables; the curtain at the Royal Opera House (#datenight).

'Just the same.' She doesn't roll her eyes; she doesn't have to. An elderly lady drifts past us, borne on the social current, and Verity intercepts her, perhaps relieved to have someone new to talk to. The old Classics teacher, Miss Balfour, famous for scorn and favouritism, is now soft, shrunken and colourless, as if she has been put through a boil wash. It's evident she can't remember either of us. Vague pleasant noises are made in response to Verity's chatter, but Miss Balfour's attention is on her jam tart. A crumb of pastry comes to rest on her bosom.

According to the clock over the serving hatch, it's nearly four. There's a train in half an hour. I look for Jean, wondering if she's ready to leave, but she's refilling at the urns, deep in conversation with one of the governors.

It comes to me as the second hand crawls over the numerals: I do not have to stay. There's no obligation to linger in this stuffy room, its panelling covered with the names of pupils who once distinguished themselves at cricket or debating. No one will notice or care if I edge away and dart down the changing-room steps, following the old path that surely still runs past the football pitch and tennis courts, through various fields, across a footbridge, into town. At Station Parade I could stop at the little off-licence for a chilled tin of ready-mix G & T, and when the train comes I could slip into a window seat and watch the town vanish, the streets giving way to woods and soft hills, yellowing meadows edged with thick margins of shadow; and, from time to time, the sudden adrenalin spike of a spire. It was a shock to me earlier today, the prettiness of the journey. But back then, we didn't notice the scenery. If we looked at the windows, it was to see our reflections.

All these people, the Jeans and Dribblers and Veritys and Miss Balfours: what are they to me, anyway? Who was I, when I was here? For a moment, I force myself to remember how it felt, to take a tray and run it along a rail, pointing at things you thought you might be able to eat, and to carry it through to a table set with bowls of ketchup and clumped white sugar. You lived in fear, entering the dining hall, of dropping your tray. If you dropped your tray, everyone screamed and clapped and chanted your name, as if this was fine entertainment.

So I will leave, because this time I can. No need to interrupt Jean; I'll send her a text once I'm out, saying I'm making my own way back to the station. Now I offer my farewells to Verity and Miss Balfour, murmuring and smiling, and then I begin to press through the scrum towards the exit, anticipating the relief of escape. A pale face turns and I glimpse the ghost of Clare Snape. Curiosity flares and is doused by expediency, because the clock is ticking and the door is within reach. So I push on, as if I haven't recognised her.

Someone puts a hand on my arm. 'Wait, wait,' Sookie Utley says, narrowing her eyes. 'Don't tell me, don't tell me, it's on the tip of my tongue.' She closes her eyes for a moment, then opens them with a snap. 'Ah – it's gone.'

'Ruth,' I say. 'Ruth Saving. We were in the same French class?' I realise I haven't even pretended not to know who she is.

'I know *that*,' she says. 'Ruth Saving. Yes – of *course*.' Still that half-croak catch in her voice, the hint of fluff on the 's'. *Thaving. Yeth of courth.* Her hand stays on my sleeve, and this is charming and also quite the opposite. All those years ago, an approach like this would have sounded a warning. It would have signified the risk of some offhand humiliation. I was wary of people like Sookie Utley.

Sookie says, 'You used to lend me your essays, you had beautiful handwriting,' and this – that she does have a sense of who I am after all; also, I was always proud of my handwriting – is unexpected and somehow affecting. Sookie Utley sidling up to my desk in the library, yawning, smelling of Marlboro reds and Rive Gauche, asking to borrow my notes on *Le Grand Meaulnes* as if bestowing a tremendous favour. Of course, I was craven and flattered, as she expected me to be; and the essays, when they were eventually returned, were the worse for wear, warped and stained with Venn diagrams left by cans of Coke and mugs of instant coffee.

I'm so flustered that when a tray of iced buns is presented to us I take one. 'Oh, no – not for me, thanks,' says Sookie, so I experience shame and find myself making some excuse or other, saying – lying – that I missed lunch. Sookie asks if I've stayed in touch with lots of people. 'Not many. One or two,' I say, swallowing a dry mouthful of bun. I would like to lick my fingers. 'What about you?'

Hardly anyone. She tells me she's just back in the country after several years in Hong Kong, they've spent most of their married life abroad so she's completely out of the loop. That's why she came today; she thought it would be fun to catch up with the old crowd. It's a pity more people didn't turn up, isn't it? There seemed to be quite a lot of interest, she even set up a WhatsApp group, but everyone dropped out at the last moment. Jess Carmichael, for example – do I remember Jess? (Indeed I do: kleptomania and an eating disorder.)

Sookie gives me the scoop on Jess's business empire, which began with a yoga class in Balham and now encompasses mindfulness festivals, forest bathing, organic skincare and a wellbeing podcast in which she chats to shamans and raw-food gurus. Jess was really looking forward to today but one of the twins came down with suspected measles – because of course Jess is anti-vax. Poor Jess, she's really pissed off.

'I'm sure she's focusing on the out breath,' I murmur and Sookie glances at me, and then she laughs, and her laugh still sounds as if it is taking her by surprise, and I bask in the warmth of it, the whole room made curious about the amusing thing I must have said.

She asks what I do, and I tell her, and when I bounce the question back she doesn't pretend, she wistfully tells me what I already know, which is that she used to write health and beauty features, and for a while was the deputy editor on a mid-market weekend supplement, but gave it up when they went to Kuala Lumpur. She was doing OK freelancing – she had a column, The Expat Files, which she kept up for a bit after Ava and Finn came along. But now everything has changed. All her contacts have disappeared and most of the magazines she worked for have gone under. So she's looking for a new direction. She did a blog for a while, first in Kuala Lumpur and then in Shanghai, a sort of insiders' guide, spas and bars, but it ran out of steam. People keep telling her she should be TikTok-ing or podcasting or setting up a Substack, midlife mojo inspo, that kind of thing, but to be honest she has quite a lot on her plate at the moment, trying to find somewhere for them to live. Just for a moment I glimpse her panic, the sense that she's in freefall, and then she leans in close and says, sounding rather shocked at herself but powerless, too, as if it's out of her hands, 'I don't know what's come over me, I haven't smoked for years, but I would absolutely kill for a cigarette.'

'It's being back here, it's a time portal,' I say, and I can see that lands, she feels the same. So I tell her I saw Dribbler smoking outside. 'Oh, thank God for Dribbler – some things never change,' she says, and as I search for him in the crowd my eyes pass over Waxham in conversation with Verity, who is dimpling and arranging her hair with a little shake, and Jean, who has spotted us and is beginning to press through the crush, eager for the reunion with Sookie Utley. Where the fuck is Dribbler? 'Ah – there he is, just behind you,' I say. 'I'm sure he won't mind.'

'He smoked enough of mine back in the day,' says Sookie, and then she asks, almost shyly, if I'll keep her company, 'for old time's sake,' as if this was how it used to be: the two of us arm in arm, strolling up to the Witch Wood or behind the Bakehouse, our heads bumping as we bent to dip stale Silk Cuts into a tiny flame.

Sure, I say. Why not.

* * *

Dribbler gives Sookie two cigarettes and then – in an archaic gesture of chivalry – he tears off one of the matchbox strikes and hands that over, along with some matches. I think he'd like to be asked to join us, but it doesn't occur to Sookie. I can't say I mind. Maybe I want her all to myself.

There's nothing to stop her. She could light up anywhere she wanted: on the Meadow, on the library steps, in the courtyard in front of the head's office. We certainly don't have to go all the way up to the Witch Wood but she says she wants to, for sentimental reasons.

It always felt as if the woods were miles away, quite beyond the normal orbit of the school, but in fact they're barely any distance at all, at the end of the track that leads past the Bakehouse and the Old Piggery pottery studio. So close, in fact, that at break time staff must have been able to see, and smell, the smoke billowing from the treeline.

Afternoon sunshine falls across the bare churned field like syrup, birds clacking into the air as we climb the stile. A few steps into the wood and it's cool and dim, very still, so the noise of dry sticks snapping underfoot sounds monumental.

We come to a little clearing, which Sookie remembers as a popular snogging spot. I refuse the other cigarette. 'Suit yourself,' she says, striking one of Dribbler's matches. She inhales and, on the out breath, steadies herself on a low branch: 'Woo. Bit of a head rush.' She hasn't really smoked since university. It was always the subterfuge and adrenalin that she was hooked on – the possibility that at any minute a chemistry teacher might erupt from the bushes – rather than the nicotine itself. With the excitement removed from the equation, with no sanction (ill health seemed so remote to us then, far less likely than nuclear Armageddon), cigarettes lost their appeal.

Sookie stands in the clearing, smoking and chattering about herself, and her certainty that I will listen is, I will admit, a tiny bit disappointing. I could be anyone, really. She just wants an audience. I look at her (the successful audacity of that sleeveless top, her legs in expensive jeans still bandy and just a smidgeon too short) and I think, *you miss the excitement, don't you? You felt so alive here.* She takes another drag, shudders and drops the cigarette underfoot, saying, *ugh, revolting, filthy habit, what was I thinking?*

The sentinel lines stretch away beneath the canopy, creating a space that is both grand and intimate. Sookie falls silent, and for some reason I assume she is having a sad thought, but then she asks if I remember the flashers. 'God, this place was absolutely crawling with them! Jumping out of bushes, waving it around.' Flashers were simply part of life back then, weren't they – like *TOTP* every Thursday in the TV Room, and bus conductors, and punks on the King's Road.

She remembers one flasher in particular: blue anorak, side parting, natty little 'tache. She and Jess called him 'the dentist'. He wasn't frightening – just ridiculous, tiresome, disgusting. People, men, are so peculiar. She and Jess whistled the 'Finger of Fudge' jingle whenever they saw him through the trees. It didn't seem to put him off.

One Saturday afternoon when she and Jess went down to Crowfield for tea at the Cartwheel and to stock up on trash mags and face masks, they saw him coming out of WH Smith's with a lady in a headscarf. When he spotted them he steered his wife into the shopping precinct, so they followed, just for a laugh. They could see his panic as he rushed ahead, monitoring their reflections in the shop windows. 'I don't know why we followed them, I don't know what we were planning to do. They went into the Safeway car park and they got in a car and sped away. I flicked him a vee as he drove past and I could see his wife was appalled, *dreadful girls, that awful place*, and Jess made a note of the number plate, very *Cagney & Lacey*, but we didn't report him or anything. Seemed to do the trick, though. We never saw him again after that.' She shivers. 'I'd almost forgotten. Disturbing, really. I would freak if something like that happened to Ava. And yet at the time it was just a bit of a joke.'

My phone pulses: a call from Jean. I shut it off, slide it back into my pocket, ask another question. Both of her children are away, boarding; oh no, this place was never really a consideration, a bit too free-form, too boho for Murray. He was sent somewhere more traditional, and that's what he wanted for them: uniforms, rules, single sex ('thingle thexth') – a *system*. He thinks it's safer.

Of course it took a while for the kids to 'bed in'. It's never easy at the beginning. Oh, it was agony for Sookie to let them go. Absolute torture. But there wasn't a choice, given all the travelling, the chopping and changing. The kids had had enough of making friends and then having to say goodbye and starting all over again. They both asked to go! Very much their idea. And thankfully they're both thriving at their respective schools now: the continuity, the activities and facilities, the friends on tap 24/7. Ava's passionate about drama and art, and Finn's sporty, competitive, *such a boy* – on all the teams. They totally know how to deal with boys there, they basically treat them like dogs, big helpings and loads of exercise, they really wear them out. Finn's terribly happy. They both are! So happy, in fact, that neither of them show any interest in switching, even though Sookie is back in London now with all these excellent day schools on the doorstep, while Murray wraps things up in Hong Kong. In fact, just getting Finn up to London at weekends is a bit of a struggle. So many match fixtures.

'They have their own lives, you see,' Sookie explains bravely. 'And knowing they're so happy is everything, isn't it? It seemed rather selfish, to whisk them away, just when they've put down roots.'

'Absolutely,' I say, and she holds up her hands, as if surrendering, or fending something off: 'I know I sound defensive, but I am so *tired* of having to explain it now we're back in the UK. So easy to judge. But of course *you* get it. I don't have to explain it to *you*.'

As we come out of the wood the sun is dipping to the horizon, shadows slanting across the fields. Sookie finally remembers to ask if I have any children, so I tell her a little about Elizabeth and where she is studying, and then she asks if I'm married. I explain Robin is a historian who is spending a few months in Basel, sifting through material on the early-modern witch trials.

She wants to know where we live. Turns out it's not a part of London she's familiar with. It was quite a hasty decision to come back from Hong Kong, it seemed to make sense to tie that in with the beginning of term, and fortunately her parents' pied-à-terre near Baker Street was empty: terrifically convenient, for sure, but tiny, and not really her style. Rag-rolling in the hallway, knick-knacks everywhere. Storage heaters! But the mews house is only a stopgap.

She's sucking up to estate agents in some of the swankier postcodes (not that she phrases it like that, of course); she's working on the assumption they'll be based in London for the next few years, though there's a chance Murray's firm will transfer him to south-east Asia. She hopes it won't come to that. London has a lot going for it. It's good to be home.

As we pass the Bakehouse we startle a boy and a girl who pull apart and flee towards the trees, looking sheepish. This reminds Sookie of getting busted sneaking back into the boarding house after a nocturnal tryst with Toby Everden. I hear her confidence that this anecdote – this prattle – will hold my attention, and this is both annoying and amusing.

We walk back past the music school and towards the Meadow. The sun has moved off the tousled grass, and most of the teenagers have gone too, though their music comes at us from the open windows of dormitories, studies and common rooms, a pile-up of beats and rhythms, different times.

The afternoon visitors are straggling towards the car park. Sookie doubles back to the Wye Building to collect her jacket while I wait by the library steps, checking my phone. Two missed calls from Jean, and a text: *Tried to ring you a few times, I'm heading off now, giving Clare S a lift – sorry to leave you in the lurch! Let's catch up properly when I'm next in London.*

The metallic pinkish-mauve shroud suspended from the clock tower flutters and rustles in the breeze, catching the last of the light. I'm standing there, looking at it, when a person comes up behind me: 'Some enterprising soul climbed up there last night. Ground staff couldn't find the cherry picker in time.'

I know who it is before I turn around, displaying my ghastly smile. On his way home but in no particular hurry, Waxham has time on his hands, certainly enough to spend a few moments sharing a joke with a visitor from the vague past. Rolling forward on his toes, then back on his heels, that familiar sailor ballet, he describes various comical attempts to get it down before the visitors arrived. He doesn't say what 'it' is, and I do not ask, though I can guess. It's such a surprise to find myself standing here with him that I forget to be flustered. It feels quite natural, really. I laugh, as I am expected to, because he is making an effort. *Once*, I think, *once I took a swig of your prescription mouthwash and held it in my mouth for a moment or two, for as long as I could bear – disgusting, but worth it, to be closer to you. I spat aqua froth into your bathroom sink and rinsed it away and saw my wild face in your mirror, and I barely knew myself.*

It's obvious he does not remember me, not specifically. I'm just someone who spent a few years here, long ago – one of many half-strangers on a sentimental journey. I mention the dressmaking dummy that was hoisted up there, in Mr Trickett's anorak. 'Ah, that must have been before my time,' he says, and I want to say: no, no, it absolutely wasn't, but I let it go.

I didn't leave a trace. This is both terribly disappointing and a great relief. 'Things change, things stay the same,' he says, sweeping hair off his forehead. 'Adolescents, particularly. So much creative energy, shall we say.'

'Lovely music today,' I say, and he dips his head appreciatively, a modest acknowledgement, and asks if I have far to travel.

'Back to London,' I say.

'Oh, well, then, you must take one of these,' he says,

pulling a roll of flyers from his jacket pocket, and with this movement something is dislodged and flutters to the grass by his feet. I examine the flyer while he stoops for the fragment of card and tucks it away. 'Piano recital, a fundraiser for the music scholarship scheme: Martha Owembe, a recent music scholar. A rising star, according to Petroc Trelawney – perhaps we'll see you there,' and off he goes (that cheerful gait, the hair of which he is so proud lifting in the breeze) past the Humanities fishpond, where once, long ago, I stuffed pebbles into the toe of a bronze Capezio ballet slipper and threw it into the rushes.

When Sookie reappears, I don't mention my interaction with Waxham, because it's ludicrous, absolutely ludicrous, and I don't know her well enough, and anyway it was so long ago, and now I've spoken to him I can see it doesn't mean anything, he's just a perfectly pleasant man in the final stretch of middle age, with eyes that crinkle rather attractively when he smiles.

And part of me wants to keep it a secret, keep him to myself, as I always did.

Sookie heard it was a giant helium penis. Taking my arm, an easy yet thrilling gesture, she says some kids put it up there in the middle of the night. 'They couldn't get it down in time for the service, but the head of games went up on a ladder with telescopic loppers and managed to deflate it.' Yes, she remembers the episode with the dummy in Mr Trickett's anorak. It was Toby Everden's idea, he made Dumbo Gunn – the smallest boy in his dorm – shin up there at 3 a.m., and didn't Dumbo fall off and break his arm? This rings a bell. I can even picture Dumbo. His real name was Colin. His ears weren't even that big. He directs commercials now. He won some award for his campaign for Heineken.

'Where's your car?' Sookie asks.

I say I came down by train.

'Well, I'm driving back, if you want a ride,' she says. 'I could drop you off somewhere near the Tube, once we get into town.'

'As long as it's no trouble... someone offered to give me a lift to the station, but they seem to have left already.'

'Who was it?' she asks, and I find I don't particularly want to say Jean's name to Sookie Utley: I'm pretty sure it won't mean anything to her, and that in itself will mean something. 'Oh, no one,' I say. 'But yes, that would be great, thanks,' and now I'm looking forward to getting in the car with Sookie, a car that will be huge and high and comfortable, the sort of luxurious monster favoured by well-to-do saviours of the planet, along with gas-guzzling AGAs and woodburners that belch out toxic particles. And more than this: I like the idea of spending more time with her, because despite her self-involvement she seems friendly, and also rather unmoored, maybe even a little lonely, and that's quite a compelling combination. Perhaps she could do with a friend like me.

The car park has emptied out, a mouth of missing teeth. Sookie is digging in her bag, looking for her keys, when her phone rings (the opening bars of 'Single Ladies'). She excuses herself and walks off to take the call, standing by the fence with her back turned, her long shadow stretching away over the field. When she comes back, she's so sorry, something has come up, very last minute, a friend who lives locally has suggested a quick drink. Of course, she can still drop me at the station, if that helps.

'Is it out of your way?' I ask, and she hesitates, just barely, before saying, 'Not really, no – not at all,' so I say, 'Don't worry, I'll walk, I could do with the exercise.'

'You sure?' she says. 'I feel awful,' but she's eager to get rid of me now, she's already moving on to the next thing. 'So good to see you again, let's stay in touch,' and then she presses her cheek against mine, once, twice; the cigarette, face cream, the faint memory of Annick Goutal spritzed on hours earlier.

In a few moments, I am walking along the grass verge approaching the war memorial when a gleaming anthracite SUV drives past, Sookie Utley high up at the wheel, Boadicea in her chariot. She doesn't slow down or wave or acknowledge me in any way. Her mind is elsewhere.

It's almost dark by the time I get home. I let myself into the hall and, by the brothy illumination of the eco-bulb, check the junk mail left out by the fabric orchid, which is Carlos's valiant attempt to civilise the common parts. Squeezing past Paul's bike, its handlebars curled like rams' horns, I unlock the door to the flat.

I've taken to leaving the kitchen radio on low when I go out, because I've found it takes the edge off the return. Various absences hang in the air like woodsmoke. When Elizabeth is here, she barricades herself behind a series of defences: doors, screens, earphones. You might imagine there's not that much to miss. But there's a specific quality to her not being here. The silence is quite different.

As I take off my coat, there's a vibration from the hall, a rattle as someone is buzzed in from the street, and then I hear the timpani of footsteps hurrying upstairs. Carlos and

Paul must be having friends round. It is, after all, Saturday night.

I pour a drink and check the fridge. On the radio they're discussing Ancient Egyptian funerary customs and the role of shabti dolls but I'm not in the mood so I switch over to the crackpot babble of a phone-in: angry people, lonely people, people with a need to be heard. While the soup heats up, I go through to the sitting room, putting my glass down on the side table and wondering where I've left the TV remote. I reach out to turn on the lamp and, as my fingers find the peg at its neck, I suddenly know, with absolute certainty, that it will happen again, and so I am spared the shock when it does, when I press the peg and the room – the cushions, the rug, the gaps in the bookshelves – leaps and blooms in the flare for one spectacular, freakish moment. And then the filament blows and the bulb dies and the shadows rush back like a flood, filling the corners of the room, settling once more in the folds of the curtains and the place where his books used to be.

* * *

I am gazing listlessly into the deep-freeze coffins when someone rams my trolley and says with aggressive forbearance, 'So sorry, could you possibly—?' Glancing up, I see Gretchen Armitage's expression snapping from assassin to hail-fellow-well-met as she locates my name and hastily assembles the other known elements of my identity.

Our daughters were friendly for a term or two at primary school, so we had the occasional glass of wine in the other's kitchen, and Gretchen and her husband Francis once recruited us to their pub-quiz team, though our performance must have been disappointing because they never asked again. Nowadays I watch Gretchen from a distance as she posts pictures of Issy's Oxford college (#proudmama) or powers across the Heath towards the Tumulus, ponytail jouncing in synch with her dog's tail.

Around the time of secondary transfer, with all its emotional redundancies, many of the mothers bought compensatory cockerpoos. It was considered a particular badge of intimacy if you and your friends obtained puppies from the same litter, via the same approved breeder. I seem to recall Gretchen's Patsy (or Betsy?) is sister to Mavis (Mabel? Avril?), who is owned by our cohort's queen bee: Shefali Wearing, the cake-stall martinet. A long time ago Shefali ran a cold eye over my gingerbread men and, with conspicuous reluctance, found them a place at the back, behind Judith Taplow's corporeal fairy cakes.

Gretchen and I exclaim and clutter up the aisle, getting in the way while people huffily reach past us for petit pois and puff pastry. We compare notes on the girls, and touch briefly on our professional lives, and Gretchen, who is in marketing, says Francis keeps being promoted and is superfrazzled. He works at the *Mail*, a bit icky but we don't dwell on that. As she speaks, I can see her remembering that dismal thing about me, a bad penny falling into a slot; and now she gets back into position behind the trolley, saying, 'Must get on and find redcurrant jelly – I've left him in charge of the lamb.' We agree to do coffee soon – it'll never happen – and she hurries off to Condiments.

She remembered something, and it wasn't the redcurrant jelly. Out of delicacy, squeamishness or fear, she did not mention Robin. She decided not to run the risk of emotion, because she has her schedule, people are coming for lunch and the lamb is in the oven. Or perhaps she simply did not know what to say. Perhaps she thought she might make it worse for me.

I complete the circuit, briefly inspecting gift boxes of scented soap I cannot justify buying, and remembering to pick up more bulbs – bayonet and screw – and then I wait my turn at the checkout. When the cashier begins to scan the eggs and celery I slide the trolley through so I can pack the items, quickly dropping the bags in so they hide the boxed soap underneath. An innocent mistake. Could happen to anyone.

At home, I peel the cellophane away and lift the soap from its nest of tissue paper. The bar smells of blossom and sunshine. I put it in a saucer by the kitchen sink. Robin preferred liquid soap, saying it was more hygienic.

In the afternoon, while my neighbours return from Sunday lunches, or head off in twos or threes for walks, I sit down at my desk, to think about steep valleys filled with crystalline air and the chink of cowbells. I find the words for other people. For the most part, the words are utilitarian: careful and precise, but colourless. Budget airlines, small academic presses, engineering companies and legal firms hire me to translate information, often quite dry and technical information. There is little call for personality, though sometimes – as with this particular job – some atmospheric hyperbole is appropriate.

In the early years of my marriage, I was quite sought after for literary translation: slim volumes for the most part, novels that would sometimes merit a nice notice in the broadsheet books sections. Though I was once shortlisted for a prize, only the most scrupulous reviewers took the trouble to mention me by name. Back then I did not mind, or not very much. The most accomplished translators are the ones you do not notice. Unobtrusive, even spectral, they do best in other people's shadows. So I thought of myself as a modest woodland plant (not a hellebore – some kind of fern), and I enjoyed the challenge of being in service to the narrative voice, evoking its particularity, its tics and rhythms, while always staying alive to what lay beneath. It was a loss when these commissions dried up around the time of Elizabeth's birth. But someone cheaper and faster must have come along. Editors retire, move elsewhere or lose their jobs.

So that is in the past, yet somehow I keep afloat, trying not to think about AI, the fin in the water. My current project is online marketing content for one of my more dependable clients, a budget airline with a new route into Bavaria. Canoeing and grassy mountain trails, with breaks for whey baths, pretzels and white sausage. The note I'm striking here is hearty and wholesome. I could do it in my sleep.

When I am satisfied with the paragraph on King Ludwig's fairytale castle at Neuschwanstein, I take a break. Waiting for the tea to steep, I check the items I'm selling on eBay (his waxed jacket has four new watchers) and then I allow myself a quick hit of Instagram, because I need the rocket fuel of some virtue signalling, a crappy aphorism, a blood-boiler hashtag or two. I always have a hunger to see what they've been up to. All these characters: old friends, cousins, people I knew vaguely at university, movie stars, the wives of celebrity chefs. I scroll through their posts as they show me their best lives, and yes, I despise them for it, for their clamorous desperation to be seen.

Look at me, look at me.

I look. I can't stop looking. Are they spilling over with guile, or entirely lacking it? I am never sure. There they are, ceaselessly insisting on the fact of their existence, imagining someone might give a fuck about their dog, their children's exam results, the Spanish Steps, a colander of blackberries on a wooden kitchen table (#blessed #lovemylife #delish). I do give a fuck, of course; but the wrong sort, not the kind they expect to solicit. Too bad. Beggars can't be choosers. No, I never post. I lurk. I am the audience, transfixed, eyes shining in the darkness. After all, if someone wants to be seen, someone else must watch. These people with their brunches and sunsets: they are nothing without me. That's the way it works.

Not much is going on today. The Janssons are in Barcelona for the weekend. Jo Upshaw has been swimming in the river downstream from her listed mill. Shefali Wearing is harvesting her lavender. Shefali likes to chronicle the turn of the seasons in Upper Holloway. Soon she will arrange gourds in a bowl, then she'll craft a wreath from eucalyptus and velvet ribbon, and in early spring she will whizz up pesto using wild garlic foraged from an Archway housing estate. *Did you go through it for needles?* That's the sort of comment you mustn't type underneath. In any case I never comment, I never say anything. A comment would give me away, and I wouldn't want Shefali to know that I'm here, taking an interest in her ambitious knitting, the Seville oranges she boils up in copper pans, her habit of typing praying hands under posts by Michelle Obama.

A youthful Jess Carmichael, emerging from Chelsea register office with a man whose head is ducked against the rice. *Fifteen years married to my best friend! Haven't stopped dancing yet!*

Because I don't like any of it, I don't 'like' any of it, and this tiny act of resistance provides the usual dopamine hit. I click to update the feed and a new picture loads: Sookie Utley has posted a photo of her feet, which are slender and tanned, in orange wedge sandals. You can just see the cuffs of her jeans at the edge of the crop. She is standing on grass and daisies, slightly pigeon-toed, in a wash of sunlight. Her toenails are painted the hot-pink of an indigestion remedy. The caption reads: *Last outing of the year for these #tenlittle piggies please don't take my sunshine away! #keepthesummergoing #everylastdrop #resist #happySunday*

I refresh the page. Now she has nineteen likes, several heart-eyes and a pile-up of crying-with-laughters. *Miss you xxx* people write, and *Toes as gorgeous as the rest of you* and *OMG need that polish!* A banner flashes up on my screen, another text from Jean, saying she was sorry to miss me yesterday, hopes I got home safely.

My phone ran out of juice – so sorry I couldn't find you to say goodbye, I message back. *Let's have lunch next time you are in town.*

While I drink my tea, Sookie posts again, identifying the nail polish (OPI, Pink Flamenco). It's funny to think of her on the other side of London, in her parents' pied-à-terre behind Selfridges, sending out these small digital pulses to remind us she's still here, frantic for the attention of people she once partnered in a tennis tournament. Waving, drowning. I click onto Google and have an aimless look for the cork wedges. I can't justify the outlay, but in a furtive rush I find the nail polish on a discount and place an order.

I carry my cup of tea out into the garden. The weight

of the honeysuckle has torn it away from the fence, and something is eating the apple tree. We always planned to do things with the garden: we talked about a water butt and raised beds, a big stone table for entertaining. A long time ago I had pictured myself sitting there, passing round bowls of olives as the light went out of the trees.

That first summer when I was pregnant we bought a green plastic table set from Homebase as a stopgap, to tide us over until we could afford something nicer. The table was always wobbly on the paving, but for various reasons we never got around to replacing it, just as we never got around to the other things, the water butt and the raised beds. The fire pit.

I don't know if I will still be living here this time next year, so there's not much point in doing anything about the honeysuckle or the apple tree.

At the end of the garden, in the dusty light filtering through the leaves, I stumble over a tray of seedlings left in the scraggly grass: ten dry plugs, running with woodlice. Picking up the tray, I remember Robin coming back from the garden centre last spring with plans to plant a line of dwarf lavender along the path. I have a clear memory of saying that would be nice for the bees – because I'd just been listening to a programme about bees on the radio – while thinking that would also be nice for me, for us. I didn't think of it as a good sign; that wouldn't have occurred to me, not then. But now I wonder what he meant by it, and how humiliated I should be, by my small humdrum fantasy of pegging out a line of laundry and then stooping to pinch the purple beads between my fingers.

He must have known by then. He must have been almost sure. And yet he went to the garden centre and bought some plants, and then he left them in the grass and forgot about them.

The houses have their backs to me. It's an unlovely aspect, harum-scarum: the irregular jumble of roofs and chimneys, the wonky lines of drainpipes and gutters scrambling over the storeys where people have built out or up. Looked at from this angle, the houses suggest neglect, even abandonment. Held together by improvisation and bodge-jobs, they have nothing in common with the prim formal facades presented to the street.

In the depths of next-door's shrubbery, the sudden violent disturbance of cats. A shadow moves over a window in Paul and Carlos's flat. I wonder if they can see me, if they are watching me. I think of them standing there, heads together, speculating. The thought that they might be feeling sorry for me, wondering if they should invite me up for a drink, makes me want to break things.

I carry the seedling tray into the kitchen and cram it in the bin, and then I try phoning Elizabeth, who does not answer her mobile. I send a message – *just checking in, give me a ring, love you* – hoping it doesn't make her anxious, because I don't want her to waste time worrying about me. I wonder what she's doing, finding her own way in a new city, and while I'm doing this the landline rings: my mother, regular as clockwork. I leave it. I'll call her tomorrow.

Robin always made omelettes on Sunday nights – it was the one night he cooked – and I haven't had the wit to think of an alternative, so I beat eggs and grate cheddar into a bowl. It's enough of an achievement, sometimes, just to get through the day.

Lying in bed later, about to turn out the light, I check Monday's weather forecast, and then, because it has been bothering me, I go back on Instagram and scroll down until I find Sookie's post. I hesitate for a moment, and then I click the heart, so it fills up with red. It feels like the right thing to do. It's friendly. Generous. Uncomplicated. I hope it pleases her. I hope she notices.

* * *

There's a notification waiting for me first thing: Sookie has asked to follow my locked account. I've only posted one picture (a large woolly cobweb strung in a tree in the park, part of some local art initiative) and I only have twenty followers (a sprinkling from the school-gate cohort; my sister-in-law and niece; my oldest friend Nell, a glaciologist currently somewhere in Chile, who loathes this site as much as all the others, and would delete her profile if only she knew how). I accept.

I will confess that the thought of this new connection with Sookie is a distraction, a pleasing private joke as I do my lengths in the municipal pool and unpin my hair and dress and walk home to King Ludwig's castle. Like the encounter with Waxham, it's a small but significant event, a reminder that some things do get easier with age. The sun is clear and strong, shadows falling sharp as knives on the pavement. Pointed yellow leaves are drifting out of the trees and over parked cars, swirling along the gutters.

Mike the window cleaner arrives mid-afternoon. The booking was made months ago, I'd forgotten he was coming, but it seems fortuitous, a good day to see more clearly. I make him tea and ask about the usual things: his little boy, where they went on holiday this year. As I put the milk back in the fridge, Waxham's flyer falls to the floor. I pick it up and anchor it beneath the clog magnet we bought in Amsterdam.

'Everything all right with you?' he says, folding up his cloths, and I could tell him now, if I wanted to, but I don't, so I just say, 'Oh, you know, same old, same old,' and hand over the cash and he goes away. It's entirely possible that he hasn't noticed. It's not as if there's anything particular to see.

* * *

I make sure I have 'read receipts' turned off before opening her WhatsApp. There's no need for her to know I've seen it. After all, I might have lots on.

Hiya I need your advice

I wait for a few luxurious hours before sending a cheery, keen-to-help reply.

She's got a house-viewing 'in your neck of the woods' and would love some local intel. She suggests we grab a coffee.

I should really say no. The Bavaria material is off my desk, making way for the pharmacy chain CEO's annual report. But it's always exactly as turgid as the previous year, and I have a few days to play with.

Let me see if I can switch some things around
Oh don't go to any trouble
No problem! I'll get back to you asap

The house in question may be less than two miles from my flat, but it's in a street that is, in other significant ways, as far from mine as the moon. I suggest meeting at the café on the high street, a boutique bakery favoured by mothers socialising after prep-school drop-off, women so hot on self-denial that they choose to gather among the cannoli and cinnamon rolls, getting off on the scent of icing sugar. Sookie will like it there.

It's a warm autumn morning, and the buggies surge along the pavement like an armada, the nannies heading to the playground, or story time at the library. I order at the counter and settle myself outside, under the awning. I'm slightly early by design – this way I can secure the best seat, prepare, ready myself – but the minutes tick by, five, ten, and I feel my advantage leaking away like the heat of my coffee. Perhaps she has forgotten. Perhaps I've muddled the date. Fifteen minutes, twenty. I'm scrolling through our messages for the umpteenth time when I glance up and see her crossing the road by the bookshop: culottes, off-the-shoulder top, huge sunglasses, the ones that make me think of nature documentaries and the faceted eyes of insects. Yes, she hits the right note; she fits in here. She's making all the appropriate references and yet you can tell she doesn't take any of it terribly seriously, because Sookie has always understood it's important not to try too hard.

She waves and picks her way towards my table, laughingly negotiating dog leads. For a moment as she looms over me I can see my tiny reflection in her glasses, hair blowing across my face, my hand going up to pull it away. I can see myself abandoning my resentment, because her smile is so broad and vivid, so confident I will forgive her, or that there's nothing, really, to forgive.

The table clatters as she dumps her phone, her car keys, the insect glasses. She's so sorry she's late, traffic was atrocious and parking a nightmare, she forgets every time, it's like childbirth. So much of the city is strange to her now, and I must be used to it, but she still can't get over the shock, all the demolition, whole blocks have vanished, extraordinary holes everywhere. Whenever her mother comes up to town she wanders around in floods of tears, unable to find the chiropodist. That's one reason why Sookie's looking at property around here: a good moment to try something new. Zone one is completely dead at weekends.

So: time for a change. She's even thinking about getting a dog. Is that completely mad? She leans back to attract the attention of the boy in an apron who is clearing a nearby table. 'Can I have an espresso, just a little steamed oat milk on the side?' she says, and though there is no table service here he says he'll bring it right over.

Sookie says it seemed like an omen, running into me at the memorial; she thinks she might as well make use of me. 'That didn't sound right – but you know what I mean.' She wants to know everything about the area. Is it safe. Have I been burgled recently. The schools. She sits back as her coffee is delivered, but when I hesitantly begin to make my excuses – this isn't my neighbourhood, I'm here on false pretences – she reaches for her phone and starts to fiddle with it, as if I might not notice or mind, and then she interrupts, asking how long it'll take to walk there, she doesn't want to be late. She flashes the screen at me, to show me the address, and I peer at it, saying *it's just around the corner*. As I say this I am checking out the asking price, which is, frankly, incomprehensible.

While she fusses with her coffee and its dinky attendant jug, I keep trying to explain that these women walking around with rolled-up Pilates mats under their arms aren't my people, but she's not listening, and now her tiny cup is empty and she's waving her black card at the young man's device and asking if I'd like to come too, if I fancy it, it's always good to have a second opinion. I'm a little curious so I say, OK, *why not*. She grabs her things and rises, and as she goes I see she has missed her sunglasses, so I pop them into my pocket.

We turn down the alleyway by the organic pharmacy, skirting the buckets of hydrangeas outside the florist. The alley opens out into a tree-lined terrace, and then the houses separate and become handsome villas set back behind flaming acers and balls of box. Sookie has already looked at and discounted several properties in this leafy neighbourhood, which is so popular with rock stars, French financiers and Historic London walking tours. The gardens were too small, she says, or the houses too overlooked. I still don't know what Murray does, though really there are now only a few options left.

Marcus, the estate agent, is waiting on the front steps, between topiary lollipops. He calls Sookie 'Mrs Inchcape'. 'I've had the full briefing from Mel, so I'm absolutely up to speed. We think you'll like this place, it's rather special. We've only just taken it on, lots of interest already but you're the first to see it; Mel really wanted you at the top of the queue.'

He ushers us in, picking up the post, closing the heavy door on the birdsong. The silence is immediate, the chemical hush suggesting superb insulation and a recent industrial clean. Marcus tells us the owners have moved back to New York.

As we follow him through the reception rooms and into the kitchen, he draws our attention to the reconfigured living space, the underfloor heating, the bespoke Italian marble worktops, also the walk-in pantry, the wine fridge and double dishwashers. Surveying these indulgences Sookie's expression, it seems to me, is sceptical, unmoved.

The house is as perfect and featureless as an egg. The renovation has done away with all its domestic history, eliminating the cornicing and ceiling roses, the coloured glass, the chessboard tiles. These tasteful sunlit spaces will feel even emptier when filled with statement lamps and long sofas, the surfaces judiciously arranged with apothecary vases and three-wicked fig-scented candles. Seeing Sookie's smile, I sense it's not doing it for her. I suppose it is possible she was expecting more, for the price.

Marcus encourages us upstairs. Our stockinged feet leave stir-marks in the pearl carpet as we climb to the first floor and the second, as we move in and out of the bedrooms and bathrooms, inspecting the rain showers and his-and-her basins, the dressing room that lights up like a fridge when you open the door, so the marquetry is displayed to good effect.

Alone in one of the smaller bedrooms, I try to imagine this house with people in it: towels on the floor, piano practice, cooking smells, someone slamming a door or running a bath. It's easier to picture strangers living here than Sookie's husband and children, who seem, from her account, so remote and unknowable. At the window I look out over the grid of the neighbouring gardens, the stone benches and sundials and media sheds. The house at my back frightens me: its pale vacant rooms a reminder of how little we leave behind when we move on, for whatever reason; how soon we are forgotten. A bluebottle that has been pin-balling around the window frame falters, falls to the sill, stutters a few times, and is still.

Sookie comes in and tugs at the cupboard doors. I see

her checking herself out in the mirror. 'What do you think?' she says.

'Amazing,' I say.

'I've seen so many houses like this,' she sighs, swinging around to inspect her top from a different angle. 'They're all the same. Furniture showrooms without the furniture. I wouldn't let Murray near it. It's exactly what he wants.'

Marcus coughs politely from the floor below: he wants us to see the garden. The folding doors hiss over stone. Shallow steps lead onto the lawn, which someone has recently mown into pyjama stripes. The planting, Marcus remarks with a gesture, is very sculptural. He means no colours, no scented flowers, a high summer of fashionable bristly things, artichokes and cardoons.

'Are you related to Mrs Inchcape?' he asks me as we follow her back indoors. I say no, we are old friends.

They have a short exchange by the front door, in which she lets him down gently, *it's fabulous but not quite right for us*, and then we walk back to the street where she left her car. She asks if I want a lift anywhere; I tell her I'm fine.

She shakes her key fob at the car, which beeps meekly. 'It's no problem. Hop in.'

Leather scalds the back of my thighs. It's hot inside, sweet-smelling, like climbing into a vanilla soufflé. The doors close with a soft firm kiss. Sookie fiddles with the dashboard, boosting the aircon, switching off the radio, which was tuned to Heart.

'Another wasted morning,' she says, sidling into the traffic. 'I'm so pissed off with Mel. She knows I want a project, something I can get stuck into, I couldn't be clearer, but they keep showing me things like that.'

She talks longingly of pulling everything out and starting

from scratch with a nice blank canvas. She has so many ideas! If she could only find the right place, things could move very fast. And yet she has already told me she's not sure whether they'll stay in the UK. It strikes me that the morning has been a thing of whim and fancy for her, a way of killing a couple of hours.

Perhaps this is how Sookie lives her life, dipping in and out of various pleasurable impulses, free to indulge them without either material anxiety or a need to commit. I can't imagine how it must feel, to be accustomed to such freedom, such blazing confidence.

There is no real jeopardy, as far as Sookie is concerned. It's obvious to us both that any decision she makes will be the right one. She has no bad options. Everything will fall into place. It always does, for people like her. If the Inchcapes stay in London, she will find the house and everyone will play ball, from the sellers and surveyors and solicitors to the builders and the people who mix the paint and landscape the garden.

Murray doesn't want a project. His position is, he works his arse off, he wants an easy life. He'd live in a hotel if he had the chance. He loves hotels. The comfort and finish, thick soft towels, instant hot water when you turn the tap, people knocking quietly on the door to deliver breakfast or buckets of ice, or turn down the bed – the knowledge that everything is reliably just so, whether you're in San Francisco or Oslo or Kuala Lumpur. That's what he wants: expensive executive luxury. But Sookie will prevail. She has the vision, as well as the time. They've spent their whole married life in rentals, very nice rentals, don't get her wrong, but not to her taste. All the time she was making notes of what worked and what didn't.

Now she wants to roll up her sleeves. Rip everything out, strip it back to the bare bones, start over. Disruption can be so cathartic, don't you think.

As the car nudges through the traffic, Sookie shares her rubric. The details matter. You have to get them right. The location of power sockets and light switches. The mechanism with which a drawer slides shut. You know when the taps are set too far back so the counter's always wet? Drives her insane. In their last house, you had to stoop for all the hand towels, day after day after day, simply because some jerk fixed all the hoops too low. Her voice is loud and impassioned. I feel a flush of embarrassment, though no one else can hear her.

Sookie continues to list these small irritations that cost her so much. Her parents' mews cottage, for instance. The fridge door has to be closed before you can open the cutlery drawer. She truly believes that these tiny everyday stresses build up over time, accumulating in your system like arterial plaque, and it simply can't be good for you, can it? She expects (and she's only part-joking) someone is researching the topic right now, proving a link to autoimmune disorders, or mental health, or gut vitality – something like that.

Sookie has spent a lot of time thinking about the best ways to live. She's a bit of an expert. She knows what she wants. It's right there – touching distance. So exciting. Just has to find the right place. She pulls up outside my flat, leaning forward to check it out, making polite noises. Though she can't come in (she has an appointment, which I suspect means a Pilates session, or maybe a facial), she has time to get out her phone, to show me a particular bathtub she liked in a Parisian hotel, and also Gwyneth

Paltrow's cooker. I umm and ah obediently, despising her, despising myself; and yet at the same time (I can't help it) I am flattered that she will trust me with her lavish plumbing ambitions. That ancient Ruth is never far away; still irrepressibly craven.

But Sookie: she's in the grip of a madness, a sort of psychosis. She doesn't know she mustn't talk about £10k ovens to a stranger. But of course I am not really a stranger, am I, because we have known each other for so long; most of our lives, in fact.

Listening to her, I understand that Sookie is lost. She finds herself adrift in the city she always thought of as home, a person without a career or dependent children, and with a partner – I sense, recognising it – who is perhaps a little too absorbed by his own career, his own trajectory, absent even when he's in the same room. Really, when you put it like that, none of it matters, the culottes, the car with its leather interior, the entitlement, the monstrous self-assurance. We are both alone. So I will sit in the passenger seat as she describes some fancy tiles she wants to import from Morocco, conscious of her bug-eye sunglasses in my jacket pocket. The truth is, Sookie needs to be heard. I feel the power of her longing.

I can do that, I think, experiencing magnanimity. I can listen to her, and maybe one day she'll listen to me.

Finally, she puts away her phone and we say goodbye, an awkward hug over the handbrake while she thanks me for giving up my morning, saying she's sure – this isn't terribly convincing – I had better things to do. I assure her I enjoyed it, I always like poking around people's houses. When I come round to the driver's side, she is pulling the foil from a packet of cigarettes, the box emblazoned with warnings, a close-up of a milky eye. She makes a 'don't start' face and cracks the window. 'Slippery slope,' she says, sparking up. 'It's all your fault. You lured me to the Witch Wood. Such a bad influence.'

Again, the foolish, enjoyable sensation of being drawn close, woven into the tapestry of her life. 'I must get you over for supper one of these days,' she says, knocking ash onto the pavement. 'I'll ask Jess too. She'd love to see you.'

'That sounds fun,' I say, giving a little wave as she eases the car out into the road. My moment in the sun is over and, standing there on the pavement, I feel deflated and a little restless too, ashamed of my compliance. Once the car has left the street, I examine the sunglasses. Stella McCartney. I don't even like them particularly but it's bright, so I put them on.

There is another truth, less easy to acknowledge. Sookie has shown no interest in me. She has asked nothing, nothing at all, and I matter so little that this social imbalance – I'm reluctant to call it discourtesy, but perhaps that's what it is – doesn't seem to bother her in the slightest. It's a reminder that the protocols that governed our adolescence are still in play. Her vivid self-involved charisma; my diffidence, my quietness, my dismal lack of colour. *What's in this for me*, I think as she drives away, her car full of smoke and Kool and the Gang, and then I understand that at this precise moment her lack of curiosity might suit me rather well. It might be a relief not to have to answer questions, not to have to put a brave face on things, to be spared her embarrassment and (oh God) her pity. It might be nice, for a while, to be no more than a footnote in someone else's story.

* * *

When I say Sookie Utley got in touch after Mr Power's memorial, my mother holds a finger in the air. 'Short girl, fair curly hair?' she says, as if we're still seventeen. She must be thinking of someone else, probably Jean Pugh. 'No,' I say, 'that's not her.' On my phone, I find the *Bulletin*'s account of the memorial, and click through the gallery until I find the picture of Sookie chatting to Waxham and his predecessor as head of music, Norman Chope, whose *The Aspern Papers* recently had its world premiere at Snape Maltings.

I wouldn't have mentioned Sookie to my mother when I was seventeen, but I do so now because I am in need of a new topic of conversation, something safe and harmless to keep her at bay. There's so much I don't want to discuss with my parents. So I bring out Sookie as a distraction – not someone I knew well all those years ago, but it's nice to be back in contact. 'Was her father an art dealer?' muses my father, thinking of Verity Spackman. Humiliated I can dredge this up so easily, I say no, Sookie's father was in advertising, a founder-director at one of the big agencies.

The truth is, I haven't heard from her since our real-estate safari, though I track her high-status activities through social media: blockbuster show at the RA, Eurostar to Paris with her sister, the Last Dinner Party at the Hammersmith Apollo. She spent half-term at her parents' place in Sussex: yellow dogs to match the foliage, big fires, wild clifftop walks.

Missed these guys so much!!! she writes below two mutinous-looking teens leaning against a farm gate. The son's account is locked, but the daughter's is public: a gallery of fancy dress and tongue-out selfies.

'Oh, I am glad to hear that,' my mother says, twitching

the cushions and settling more deeply into the sofa. 'Old friends can be such a comfort.' She asks if I've heard from Nell, and I say not since she went to some remote location in Chile to study her blinking glaciers.

I haven't told Nell about Robin. I've started several emails but I can't seem to find the words, and at those moments when I long to hear her voice I've been thwarted by the time difference or a lack of signal. Nell can't be doing with social media, so she does feel very far away, almost lost. 'You must miss her,' my mother says, and she's right. I do.

My parents have been for lunch with friends in Bayswater, 'popping in' to see me before they catch the train back to Ely. They've taken to doing this recently: they're keeping an eye on me. It is a gesture of love, I know that, but the effect of being subjected to their regular sorrowful scrutiny can be quite lowering. Sometimes I feel as if they are simply waiting for me to fall apart.

I go into the kitchen and refill the kettle so I don't have to be looked at for a moment. When I return, they are both quietly gazing into their phones as people in fairytales gaze into magic mirrors or enchanted pools. My mother startles when I lean over with the teapot, and says, a little defensively, 'Just catching up! Barbara Elliott is in Lisbon for a few days. Doesn't look as if she's having much luck with the weather, poor thing.'

My father grunts in acknowledgement, though he's not really listening; he's having difficulties with the wifi. 'It seems to have logged me out,' he complains. 'Have you changed the settings?' He wants to double-check the password, which I keep pinned to the fridge door. As I remove the note, I see that Waxham's fundraiser is tonight. I was never going to go, of course.

Back in the sitting room, I begin the incantation. 'Big r, little x, little t, seven, nine, y, big y, I mean...'

'Oh, now that is such a shame,' my mother murmurs, perking up like a flower in water. 'You can see Barbara is putting a brave face on it, bless her, but the hotel seems to be in the middle of a refurb – Donald, look, you can see the builders' materials at the end of the terrace. How very unfortunate! I suppose that's the risk you take, travelling in low season. Oh dear, and the Botanical Gardens have seen better days... That's a very ragged palm... and none of the water features seem to be functioning. Poor Barbara! She was so looking forward to the break. She's had such an awful time recently, what with her hip, and the phone scammers, and then there was the business with the dog – you know it had to be put down in the end.' I sit back with a sigh and my mother snaps out of her pleasurable trance, remembering herself. 'Now, what news from Elizabeth?' She doesn't put the phone away, but she does place it face down on the cushion.

Elizabeth, I say, seems to be finding her feet. She has mentioned a few new friends – people from halls, and on her course. She's too busy to be easily contactable, but I'm taking that as a good sign.

'Can't you persuade her to set up a Facebook?' my mother asks. 'It's such a good way to stay in touch! It would be lovely to see what she's up to. No, I know the young people don't use Facebook much, it's all snap this and twit that, and then of course you hear such terrible things about mental health and cyberbullying, those poor girls pouting and putting themselves on display for everyone to see...' She says if you go on the internet and google my niece Catriona, all kinds of things come up.

'What kind of things?'

My mother's mouth pulls tight, like a drawstring. 'Oh, this and that. The things she's wearing – well, really I suppose I mean the things she *isn't* wearing... and, to be quite honest, I am shocked by some of the language they use. It's all so public! Where she's going, who she's going with... Such a lovely girl, she could be so pretty if she tried.' She and my father are wondering if they should say something to my brother and his wife. 'Isn't that right, Donald?'

My father makes a non-committal noise. He seems to be browsing wine offers and doesn't want to get involved. When I suggest it might be a bit OTT to intervene – after all, Catriona is twenty, an economics student at Warwick, captain of the university netball team for God's sake – there's a bit of back and forth but my mother's attention has begun to drift, her hand creeping out towards her phone, as if she's running out of charge and needs to replenish. Finally, she can wait no longer and disposes of the argument by changing the subject. 'Now, before I forget,' she says, picking up the phone, 'Diana Watkins – you remember Diana – posted the funniest thing the other day: I thought you'd like to see it,' and she peers and scrolls, slowly excavating her news feed, while I wait. I wonder how much time I have wasted like this, as people try to find clips on YouTube or links to great pieces in the *New Yorker* that I'll never read, and I long for the rules to be laid down, made plain to all, so that no one else can hold me to ransom like this.

My mother's keyboard clicks are turned on: cute popping sounds that set my teeth on edge.

'Ah! Here it is.' She passes the phone to me, a gift. A viral clip, several years old, of some baby pandas scrapping in a pen. 'So sweet! They made me think of Mr Perks, for some reason.' A cat, long dead, admittedly black and white. 'Lovely,' I say. 'Adorable,' and for a while we sit there while the pandas tumble.

My father finally must have placed his order, because he puts away his phone and rubs his knees thoughtfully. As he leans forward, I have a sinking feeling: *oh no*. 'Now, Ruth,' he says. 'If you don't mind us asking... how are things going with Robin?' My mother drops her phone in her bag, a signal that this is serious.

I say our solicitors are in contact, things are moving along. My mother's hands flutter at her collarbone, touching her necklace for comfort. 'I didn't know it had got to that stage,' she says weakly. 'I thought you were trying counselling.'

'Oh, no, we're past that point,' I say. 'I thought I told you this? – he's involved with someone else. I am pretty sure it's one of his faculty colleagues, and I wouldn't be surprised if it's been going on for ages. He's trying to keep it quiet – he's still going around telling everyone it's a mutual decision, no third parties. But Elizabeth has seen various things lying around the flat.'

My mother makes a sound that conveys both doubt and horror. She'll be imagining suspender belts rather than face serum and a box of tampons but I'll just leave that hanging.

'At least he's not pretending he might come back,' I say, because this is no time to mince words. 'He couldn't be clearer about that. And in a weird way, I'm grateful – there's no ambiguity.'

'But why would he say it's mutual if—' asks my mother, and I feel the rage boiling up, the misery of not being believed.

'I have absolutely no idea! I guess he thought it would play better, not only with friends, but with Elizabeth. Which is stupid, really, because she saw the whole thing.'

My mother flinches. I didn't phrase that well. What I meant was, Elizabeth was here. It happened around her. She noticed that he was absent even when he was present, and it puzzled her. Sometimes she would challenge him about it, the tuning out at mealtimes, the not paying attention. *Did you hear what I said, Dad? I literally just said that.* But I made allowances because Robin was busy, stressed, preoccupied. I let it pass.

It wasn't as if there were scenes or raised voices. No one threw anything or stormed from the room. Elizabeth only saw me cry once, and that was after he had left. Officially left, I mean, with suitcases and boxes. That evening, I started to run a bath and while the tub was filling I opened the cupboard on the landing where he kept his shirts – quite deliberately; as a sort of test. I was prepared. Yet in that moment I felt the full weight of those twenty years, and standing in front of the bare rail I wept, because I finally understood he had been leaving for months, possibly even years. It had been a long discreet process of detachment, and it crept up on me, something I could not see; could hardly bear to acknowledge, until it was cold hard fact. He no longer wanted this life. He no longer wanted me. So I cried then, and Elizabeth came out of her room and we held each other.

But I won't share this with my parents, who will not understand, who will not say the right thing. Sometimes, there is a little strength in declining to explain, in refusing to make yourself vulnerable. So I say nothing, and we sit together in a moment of silence so tremendous that I can hear someone next door on the stairs.

My mother glances at my father, cueing him in. It's a line they've rehearsed. 'Well, it's a great shame,' he says. 'We're both very upset, Ruth. We know you weren't keen on this when we talked about it last time—'

I lick my lips. Oh God. They're not going there, not again. Surely not.

'We really do feel it might be worth trying to speak to him. That is, I'd like to hear what he has to say.'

I feel the humiliating babyish prickle of tears. 'Please don't,' I say. 'It won't help.' If I felt stronger, I would challenge the vanity of my father, who has a hunch that if only he and Robin could speak, man-to-man, my marriage could be mended. But I also fear the things Robin might say when cornered. Anything to get them off his back. I fear what he might say, because it turns out I do not know him at all, and the only two things I am sure of are that he is an accomplished liar, and that he hates me. He must hate me a great deal, to do this.

'I thought I could fly out to Basel for a few days, to see if there's anything—'

'No,' I say. 'Please, no.' *Just listen to me.*

My father says, 'What you have to understand, dear Ruth, is that this is the worst thing that has ever happened to us – to your mother and me.'

The cup cooling in my hand, the lamplight on the rug, the scratch of rain at the windows. This will be one of those moments I will never forget. I've had too many of them recently. Every so often something terrible is said and it lands like a lightning strike, its sudden bleak illumination rendering the familiar landscape – all the things you took for granted – strange and frightening, quite unknown.

Perhaps when I pick over this comment in the future, I may even manage to find it comical. What marvellous lives my parents have led, how agreeable and sheltered; or otherwise, how delusional. Can it really be that so little has gone wrong for them that the banal failure of my marriage becomes the defining tragedy of theirs?

Oh, I know that is how they see it, as a failure: my failure. They will not say it to my face, not exactly, but I am aware they blame me, because at some level I am at fault. The wives always are. Recently, I've been thinking about my mother's friends Angela and Joy and Christine, women whom she never seemed quite so intimate with after their husbands left. *She let herself go. She took her eye off the ball. She would keep on with that funny little job of hers.*

'I don't have time for this now,' I say, seeing a way to get rid of them. 'I must get ready – I'm out tonight.'

'Oh, I didn't realise you had plans,' my mother says. 'You should have said.'

'Didn't I? I thought I mentioned it on the phone.'

'Oh, maybe you did,' says my mother, a little bruised, and I know she'll worry about this on the way home, what else might be slipping away from her. 'I hope you're doing something nice.'

I say it's a piano recital in Spitalfields. I have no intention of actually going.

The wind rattles the bathroom window as I stand by the sink, applying mascara and spraying scent on my wrists, wondering at the lengths I'm going to, the extent of my charade. I'll get them out of the flat and walk around the block, that's all. There's no need to change my top. I do it anyway.

Nothing else is said about Robin. We all leave together, filing out into a squall of wet leaves, the dread dark. A pizza carton slides over the pavement.

Anxious to make my escape, I say I'm going to be late, would they mind if I made a run for it? And then I'm hurrying away towards the glow of shops and takeaways, knowing the two of them will be conferring, debating my frame of mind, lamenting the situation. My plan is to duck into the Tesco Metro, buy dishwasher salt, and return home when the coast is clear. But as the tube station comes into view, I am surprised by an impulse to do what I've said I'll do. Why not? Perhaps it'll be good for me.

It's easy enough to step out of the wind into the ticket hall, which is tiled like an abattoir, and pass through the barriers, and to be carried down by the escalator; and as I come out onto the platform a train arrives, behind a gust of hot stale air, so I don't even have to wait. The doors open and close, the lights fall away, we speed into the dark. The carriage is full of people whose eyes are lit up by their screens. No one else seems to notice when another train looms up and rattles alongside for a few seconds: a glimpse of a girl fixing her make-up, a man with a tattooed neck, a woman in a red coat who looks a little like me. And then the tracks wrench us apart and the other train disappears as suddenly as it came.

OTHER PEOPLE'S FUN

* * *

'What's the name?' asks the woman at the trestle table, busy fingers poised over a tin box. Only one or two envelopes remain, because it's about to start. 'You haven't pre-booked? Ah, OK, I'm not sure if there are actually any tickets left.' She goes off to check while I fold my umbrella, and when she comes back she says I am in luck, there were a few returns. These events do tend to be terribly popular! Next time, I'd be advised to keep an eye on the head's emails and book well in advance via the school website. I press my card to the device and she says she hopes I'll stay for drinks at the end.

The church is shimmering with candles, the scent of cheap molten wax. People are obliged to shift and lift coats as I make my way to an empty seat, their conversations breaking up too: the school ski trip, UCAS dilemmas, whether it might be possible for Lara to do work experience in the summer. For these current parents, this is a social occasion, a chance to network and foster connections.

No sign of Waxham, not that I'm looking. That's not why I'm here. I unbutton my coat and sit down, dropping the wet umbrella beneath my seat. Mannerly applause as the pianist walks out and settles at the stool, arranging her music. The audience falls silent.

She places her hands on the keys, and it begins. After a few minutes, I sense my thoughts beginning to settle, like sediment in a jar. It is pleasant to sit and listen, with no other claims on one's attention. No need to think about work, unpaid invoices, Form E, the leak under the kitchen sink, the terrible thing my father said. I can put it all aside, disregard it for a short while. I can. I will.

The notes spill through her fingers in a jubilant rush, someone shaking out a bolt of silk; and then the music becomes a ribbon that takes me to a destination that turns out not to be a destination after all, but another point along the journey, one of many. Perhaps, I think, this is what an orderly mind sounds like: clarity, precision, control.

There is a stir at the end of the first movement, as people cough and shift position. For a moment a gap opens up, and there is Waxham in the front row, and then someone leans forward and he is gone. The pianist begins again. For twenty minutes, an hour, I try to believe what the music is telling me: look, there is a pattern, many patterns, and everything will be resolved in the end.

Once the applause has finally died away and the soloist has stepped down to join the crowd – relinquishing her sacred status, revealed as a pretty girl in an ASOS frock – I am buttonholed by Trudie Walsh from Outreach. Accepting a glass of wine, I let her run through her little speech about the difference these bursaries make, the transformative effect, lives changed forever, while out of the corner of my eye I'm watching Waxham passing through the crowd like a hot knife through butter, shaking hands and smiling, much hostly bonhomie. Yes, I say to Trudie, I'll certainly bear it in mind; and all the time Waxham is coming closer and closer. Keen to move on, Trudie puts a hand on his arm, drawing him into orbit, saying, 'Well, here he is, the very person! Ian –' and Waxham swings around, wearing an expression of genial confidence. His eyebrows rise in feigned delight but I can tell he doesn't recognise me from our recent encounter by the clock tower. It was only brief and I'm not memorably gorgeous or hideous.

Nothing further back.

OTHER PEOPLE'S FUN

'How splendid, now, whose parent are you?' he asks cheerfully.

'Oh, no! Not a parent. Not of – I mean, I'm an Old Girl.' As I say this, I want to die. The phrase is appalling, grotesque, horribly accurate. Trudie has made her escape and now he is marooned with me, trapped. 'What were your dates? Haha, yes, as if you're a head of state!' he says, a line he likes to trot out, and I tell him and knock back the rest of my wine, giddy with panic.

'So we must have overlapped,' he says, and I say, 'Yes, and in fact I think I babysat for your children a couple of times.'

'Really?' he says, frowning, doing some vague calculations. He still hasn't asked for my name. 'So that must have been when we were still at Flint View? The little bungalow opposite the church. We weren't there for very long – not enough room for all of us.'

'It had quite a brown kitchen,' I say, and he says, 'Oh yes, brown and orange, a bit of a period piece even then. The Franklins live there now, Jane teaches biology. It's had several Estate Office makeovers, you wouldn't recognise it.

'We were only there for a year or two before I took over as boys' housemaster and we all had to squash into Burns Flat. And then when I became director of music, we moved off-site to a house near the green. Forgive me, your name is –?'

'Ruth Saving,' I say, and then I have to stand by helpless as he tries to dredge up some memory. 'I wasn't musical, but I was a member of the choir. I think we did *Carmina Burana*? I was in the same year as Robbie Shepherd—'

Robbie Shepherd is now a famous tenor, feted for his lieder. None of us called him *Robbie* back then. As a new boy, he was heard crying in bed after lights out, and for the next seven years was known as Rob the Sob.

Waxham says, gladly, 'Ah, I remember your year very well. Marvellous Robbie, and Verity Spackman, who seems to be running the world now, Sookie Utley, and Michael Bartlett. Michael played such a key role in the vaccine's development. A remarkable year! You get them, every so often.'

Naturally, he'd remember fucking Sookie.

Waxham is chuntering on about another good vintage maybe seven years ago, which has produced a tech entrepreneur, a filmmaker whose short recently won a BAFTA, and a designer who dressed a Kardashian for the Met Gala. 'And Mono, of course.'

I say I haven't heard of Mono.

'I'm fairly sure that's his stage name now, there have been a few iterations. At school he was Kayden Salvador, a very gifted music scholar. People who know more about this than I do say his stuff is very much taking off at the moment. He stays in touch and sends me tickets every so often. I saw him perform at Meltdown last summer, quite the eyeopener.' A slight agonised pause, then he says, 'So you did some babysitting for us?'

'Once or twice,' I say. 'We all fought for those staff babysitting gigs, because it meant access to TV and a biscuit tin. I think you had two little girls?' How they fussed and bickered when I closed *Clever Polly* and snapped off the light. They always wanted more: another chapter, a last sip of water, a final trip to the toilet, the retrieval of a particular toy or scrap of dingy fabric (as precious as any martyr's shroud). They could tell I was eager to leave that small hot room under the baking roof tiles, a room where there was barely space for the bunkbed and a chair, the sun nagging away at the red curtains patterned with yellow teddy bears. 'Don't go, Ruth. One more story!'

Firmly I shushed them and went out, pulling the door so it dragged on the bristly carpet. Staff accommodation, no frills.

I have not forgotten their names. I salted them away in the secret place where I hoarded all the treasures collected during my field trips: lucky charms and mementoes, trophies, clues, portents; nuggets of knowledge that might, following some unimaginable sequence of circumstances, show him we were meant to be together. The Kim Philby biography on his side of the bed. The Herbie Hancock LPs between the Glass and the Handel. Oh, I put it all together. He bought his jumpers from M&S, his shoes from Bally. He liked Rose's Lemon and Lime marmalade, pork pies and Bell's whisky. On the toilet, he read *Private Eye* or the *Observer* magazine. The details sang with significance and I noted them all, down to the brand of shaving cream in the bathroom cabinet, the mouthwash next to the sink.

These things go through my mind while he tells me about Erica and Peggy, little girls no longer. Erica is a speech therapist in Oxford with children of her own, Peggy is a solicitor in London. He saw her last week; he's up in London a lot at the moment, working on a project with Mr Braithwaite – was Mr Braithwaite after my time? He must have been. But yes, the girls. Big family gathering last month for Carla's birthday: you remember Carla.

Carla: a slight, pale person in dungarees and collarless shirts, frenziedly wiping sticky surfaces, or dragging hawsers of laundry from the washing machine, wondering if she should cry off staff drinks because of Erica's earache. Even now, I couldn't care less about Carla. 'How is she?' I ask. The only thing that mattered about Carla back then was that he'd given her piano lessons at his previous, first, school, when she was fifteen. That was how they met. I wonder what Erica and Peggy make of that now. How does this uncomfortable fact fit into the family legend?

'Oh, she's fine, yes – very well! She will be pleased I ran into you here.' In the lull, he gestures to the pianist, holding court on the other side of the crowd. 'Do you follow Martha's career?'

'Not exactly... no; someone mentioned it, I happened to be free,' I say, but his attention has skittered away over my shoulder, *one moment, just coming*, and then he says, 'Well, you must excuse me, such a pleasure to catch up,' and he moves off, as easily as he came.

A tray comes at me and I grab another glass and empty it on my way towards the exit. I leave the glass on the trestle table, and then I start to shrug myself into my coat, dropping my umbrella in the struggle. Someone picks it up and hands it to me. In a space full of tall, shiny people, she is surely one of the tallest and shiniest. Health and wealth come off her quite forcefully, heat from a radiator.

She's making a run for it, too. She rushed here from a meeting and now she has to get to supper across town, the Uber is on its way but she's going to be hideously late. Wonderful music! She's new, so it's quite overwhelming, really.

She means, her daughter's new – just started this term. Year Nine. 'What about you?' She smiles at me, hopeful, flipping her hair over her collar. I realise she's nervous, conscious of a new hierarchy, uncertain of her position.

Suddenly my own story seems dull, so odd and pathetic,

like the top I had changed into, believing it to be chic. Where's the fun in being an Old Girl? It might be nice to be someone else, however briefly: the sort of person who wangs on about the climate emergency while taking eight flights a year. The sort of person who packs her children off to be looked after by strangers, and has any number of Stella McCartney sunglasses lying around. Maybe it would be amusing to be someone like that, for a change.

I give thanks for my Max Mara coat, a lucky find in a Kentish Town charity shop. 'Oh dear no,' I say, and I'm barely pulling rank; my seniority has scarcely occurred to me. 'We're years in. Yah, no, they've loved every minute.'

It's easy. Just a matter of standing a little taller and holding back, just a fraction. It's a matter of smiling, but not necessarily with the eyes. Courteous, but from a distance.

It's raining very hard and her Uber seems to be stuck in traffic so we wait at the top of the steps, and because there's no one to overhear us I riff a little on Ava and Finn, who are the right fit for this situation, and it feels rather like swimming in the sea, like being lifted and carried forward by a strong swell. I don't know if it's the risk or the wine or the encounter with Ian Waxham. Either way, it feels fun, a little crazy, but pleasurable.

She listens to me with a supplicant's attention as sheets of rain blow over the pavement. Patterns of light dance in the puddles, and then tyres slice through them.

She absolutely agrees, the music is terrific. Music was at the very top of their list when they were considering Mimi's education because she is quite gifted when it comes to flute and piano, and also has a remarkable singing voice.

Her expression conveys a modest awareness of this

stage-mother yakity-yak, and also a conviction that we are really talking prodigy here.

I say, quite grandly, 'Music at Howard has always been of a very high standard.'

'Oh, yes, and so much of that is down to Mr Waxham. Have you noticed much of a difference since he went part-time?'

'Not really,' I say, losing confidence. Pleased to have information I lack, she says he was very forthcoming when they spoke just now – it's a passion project, an opera about the sailor who went mad during that solo round-the-world race back in the Sixties. An English teacher who recently moved to City Boys is working on the libretto. They regularly meet up in London.

'He says it's now or never. I guess we all know that feeling! And he promised there'll be no falling off, the choir's in excellent hands with Miss Vance and the carol service will be up to its usual standards.'

She checks her phone. Her Uber's arrived, just over there. 'Hope to see you at the carols. Lovely to meet you!' Off she goes, her long gleaming boots giving her the air of a cavalry officer. I open my umbrella and as I come down the steps the adrenalin fades and I start to feel foolish, shocked that I lied to her, and that lying came so easily. And shocked, too, by the way I felt when I was with him.

* * *

Sookie is in Cape Town, where she's doing sun salutations on the beach and having al fresco lunches in vineyards with her BFFs, and then she's back in London and suggesting I come over for supper, though it's hard to pin her down to a date. I nominate one particular Thursday, a day when I'll be in town late afternoon for an appointment with my solicitor, but she never gets back to me about it, and then the day arrives.

When I come out of the solicitor's office, I wander through the streets in a bit of a daze, losing myself in bad-tempered festive crowds. The West End is bathed in an Arctic glare: the chasms between the buildings are strung with cats' cradles of blue-white LEDs, promoting a new Nike trainer or Disney film. Giant balls and streamers shimmer and wink along the avenues.

I walk to clear my head and shake off the conversation. It was very practical and matter-of-fact – I'm past the crying stage now, which makes it easier all round – and we seem to be navigating according to well-established principles, but everything feels so febrile, so uncertain. I am too old for all of this. I am too old for fear; I am too old for hate. But that's all I've got in the tank right now.

To get away from the crowds, I duck into an arcade lined with dinky boutiques selling high-end tourist tat: cashmere and chess sets, kilts, vintage watches, cigars. Two women stand in front of one shopfront, glass and brass so clean you could lick it, discussing where to find the best martini.

A bell tinkles as I push the door, the flame of the candle on the counter nodding in the draught. The interior, dense with the scent of bergamot and sandalwood, is dim, wood-panelled, quietly austere. It's modelled on a gentleman's study, perhaps, or a dressing room. One member of staff behind the counter, a well-dressed woman slightly older than me. She greets me appreciatively, as if we are old friends.

This moment – the silly fleeting thrill of being taken

seriously, even by unimportant people – is always pleasurable. The truth is I don't mind being mistaken for someone who cares about fripperies, who might decide to stock up on bath oil or hand-milled soap ('made in the ancient method by the monks of San Michele') without much consideration of the price.

The saleswoman waits attentively while I make my selection, my index finger hovering over the glass-topped counter: lilac, gardenia, orange blossom. Now she pulls out the drawer and places the fat bars of soap before me, a spectrum of whites and creams. There's no harm to it, this matter of briefly inhabiting another world. It's innocent enough.

The bell rings and a party of Japanese tourists presses in, filling the shop with carrier bags from Fortnum's and Trumper. 'Would you like a moment to decide?' the assistant suggests, and I say that's fine. Left to my own devices I sniff the bars, one after the other, wondering if I prefer the hyacinth or the gardenia, enjoying the cool smooth weight in my hand. While the saleswoman is busy with the other customers – tucking their choices into boxes, cradles filled with so many plump babies – my sleeve falls over my hand on the counter, and then as I move on I slip the box of bath oil into my pocket.

At the other end of the shop there's quite a muddle now of payment options and tissue paper and stiff carrier bags being cracked open, so I take my time, drifting along the displays, inspecting the items on the shelves. That is when I feel it: the unmistakable burn of scrutiny. I look around. One of the tourists quickly drops her gaze, as if she is almost but not entirely sure of what she just saw. At this point I take an interest in the Giardino del Chiostro candle, and then I straighten up and move to the door. The assistant catches my eye and so I say I'll have a think, I can't quite decide. The bell tinkles and I am out in the cold, walking briskly down the arcade, past the backgammon sets and the shoe-shine man who is starting to put away his brushes. In my pocket, the little box bumps against my hip.

I leave the arcade and slip into the lights and the noise, the early-evening bustle. When I am confident no one is following me, I slow down and begin to wander without purpose. I feel jumpy, alive: too alive to go home. Beyond Oxford Circus the streets quieten, the pavements speckled with raindrops. Long ago, I temped around here: holiday cover on the front desk at a travel agency and a firm of solicitors.

In another life I would be meeting someone for a drink tonight, stepping into the cosily low-lit bar of a hotel, or even one of these pubs with coloured glass glowing in the windows – the sort of place where once, long ago, Nell might have gathered us around a big sticky table to share jokes about starter jobs, dissertation set-backs and crappy flat shares. If not the most ebullient member of the group, I was an important participant, her oldest friend, the person who knew her best and was known best by her. I'm not entirely sure what happened between then and now. Nell's research took her to Sweden and Alaska, where she married someone I've never met, and then on to Chile; and my own life filled up with other things. And now I have a story to tell, I have no one to tell it to.

Suddenly I feel a longing to hear Nell's voice. Nell would get it out of me. She'd know what to say. She'd understand why the email containing my news has been sitting in my drafts folder for months. I should call her now, in case the satellites are in alignment. But then I remember the time difference. She'll be busy somewhere in the Southern Patagonian Icefield, investigating sediment plumes and surface currents. This is not the right time. I walk on.

Garden squares, mansion blocks, cream stucco terraces behind iron railings: discreetly, the architecture has become more residential, though judging by the unlit windows no one actually lives around here. Walking past a parade of tiny shops – wedding dresses, hand-painted lampshades – I realise I'm not far from the mews where Sookie is billeted. I hadn't known I was doing it, but somehow I have found my way to her. I think of her coming home (though I struggle to imagine her reason for going out in the first place: session with the personal trainer, perhaps), turning on the lights and taking off her coat, flinging herself down on the sofa, which will be navy velvet, or possibly grey linen, disconsolately scrolling through Instagram, which reminds her of all she is missing: her children, her husband, the sun. It is possible she would be glad of the company. After all, she too is alone.

I hesitate for a moment, my reflection caught next to the dummy bride, with her silk roses and the gracious, modest arrangement of her hands, then I find Sookie's details. And while the call connects I cross the road and enter the mews, a narrow cobbled lane lined with the ghosts of stables and carriage stalls, properties extensively remodelled for foreign investment portfolios. The windows are mostly dark.

The mews cottages cluster behind the Georgian squares like children hiding in their mothers' skirts. In warm weather, I've walked past and seen inhabitants gathering on the cobbles with drinks and pop-up chairs; but tonight the only movement, apart from the intensifying drizzle, is the halting progress of someone taking a tiny dog out for a shit. Sookie's phone rings and rings, and then clicks through to voicemail. I shelter in someone's unlit porch as I send a text, because messaging is what you do in these circumstances, just to explain the reason for the call, as if trying to actually speak to someone on the phone is in some way outlandish, even impolite.

Hey, I'm in your neck of the woods – wondering if you're around

There is a light on in number seven, the house that belongs to Sookie's parents – a dim square of dimpled glass in the front door – but all the windows are black. My hair's full of rain, and so are my best meeting-appropriate boots. Watermarks, for sure. Naturally, I forgot my umbrella. In this sheltered spot I wait to see if she will respond, just in case she's on her way home. Nothing. Then the thrill of the three pulsing dots, proof she's looking at my message.

The dots vanish. Then they're back again. *Ah sorry I'm out RN :(another time*

Definitely, I type. Then I slide the phone back in my pocket, feeling it knock against the box. Looking over at number seven, I catch a small movement on the upper storey, an adjustment to the quality of the darkness perhaps. Now a light comes on, a low warm light as if someone's opened a door, brighter in one window than the other. Shrinking back, I blink up into the rain, a hand as a visor. Now I can see the angle of the wall as it hits a sloping ceiling, the corner of a gilt picture frame or a mirror, the motion of a shadow. A figure appears at one window and quickly tugs the curtain across, and then does the same in the other, and she is so close I can almost hear the metal hoops scraping and jingling on the pole. I can see quite clearly that it's Sookie, wrapped in some loose thin fabric, a sheet, perhaps, or a dressing gown, something grabbed to cover herself, and she is laughing.

I draw no conclusions from the fact she said she wasn't at home. Although it would have been so easy to say, *Sorry – another time – Murray is here for a few days*. I would have understood that. It's odd she didn't mention him. But she owes me nothing, which means I don't owe her anything either.

Perhaps that's why I don't leave immediately. Perhaps that's why I stay in the shadows, my boots filling with water, the cold wet wool tight on my shoulders, my eyes fixed on number seven.

The mews is deserted, the dog walker long gone. No activity for ten minutes, fifteen. The rain eases off slightly. On the other side of the houses, the traffic pulses down Gloucester Place: buses, a siren or two. There's a beeping coupled with a robotic warning as a delivery truck backs up to the little parade of shops.

A pedestrian turns into the mews and I shrink back but his umbrella is up and his eyes are down, on the puddles. He doesn't notice me as he hurries past and lets himself in to a house several doors down.

I tell myself I'll stay until half past, then I'll give up and head home. I want to see what Murray looks like, the real Murray, not the one she puts up on social media. It's natural to be curious. Come on, I think, willing a manifestation. *Come on. Show yourself.* In number seven, a shape moves over the stippled window in the front door. A flicker of movement blocks the light for a moment, then Sookie, barefoot in jeans and a jersey, is opening the door, and a man comes out, fastening his jacket, and it's Ian Waxham.

'Watch the step,' she says in a low voice. 'I keep meaning

to get it fixed,' and Ian Waxham looks at her and whatever he sees makes him hesitate, and I glimpse her face as she holds it up to him like a flower, and yet at the same time she is issuing a silent warning, *no, the neighbours*. And honestly, in that moment she looks... so ridiculous. So pleased with herself – so pleased with herself, and so ridiculous.

They do not touch and yet in their separation there is a full pantomime of erotic longing, as if she is running her fingers along the zipper on his jacket, suggestively pulling on the hood toggles. Then Ian Waxham makes a little farewell gesture and turns and walks away, bending his head into the drizzle. She doesn't watch him go. She closes the door, shutting herself away with all the light.

I see him heading off down the mews with his North Face backpack hunchback, and it's such a dull kind of disappointment when I consider the things I felt when he raised his hands and held the silence, waiting for the choir to collect itself.

Perhaps it started at the memorial. Or perhaps it's been going on for far longer than that. Perhaps the fuse was lit when she fainted in the concert, or joined the choir, or simply passed him in the corridor. Either way, I remember standing under the oak tree, waiting as she walked away to take that call, so animated as she talked and twisted her hair, ensuring she caught the late-afternoon sunshine. It felt like a performance at the time, and I'd assumed it was for my benefit, but now I doubt that. She knew he might be watching her from the music school or looking out of the Wye Building, phone to his ear.

Only an hour ago, leaving the solicitor, I had felt a longing to be frank with someone – with her. I had allowed myself to imagine how candour might feel, how it might liberate me, and how it would be received. I wanted to show myself to her, to be seen. Now, as I follow Waxham down the mews, I think about the slippery partisan nature of truth, the way it exposes you and makes you vulnerable.

Waxham leaves the mews and crosses the road, weaving between the knots of people coming out of the cinema where pricy cocktails are brought to your recliner, as if you're flying Emirates. His untidy gait – stooped, hands in pockets, slightly shambly – is still familiar, as familiar as this old habit of surveillance.

How we fell on sightings of Waxham at school, straining to see him in the distance, yet finding ourselves unable to meet his eye when he acknowledged us in passing on the Meadow or by the changing-room steps. Cold dark winter afternoons were made thrilling because you might come around a corner to find him standing there, arms folded, telling someone to pipe down or hurry up, requisitioning you to photocopy something or babysit his children. Perhaps that was the point of choir: a period of glorious enforced staring, when you were agonisingly spared the need to be anything other than one of many.

The truth is, there was nothing else to occupy us. Without Waxham, there was only the timetable and the relentless and exhausting company of adolescents. You could leave the boys behind when you entered the boarding house, but there was no escape from the girls. The girls were everywhere: in the dorms and common rooms and study units, helping themselves to your Tampax, your favourite boots, your shampoo as you stood naked beside them in the open showers. We were endlessly tumbled together like stones at the bottom of the sea. It knocked the corners off some of us, but some of us developed flint-sharp edges.

For many of us, Waxham was a continuation of that communal experience: a mutual interest, like cigarettes, or 10,000 Maniacs, which gave your friendships a richer emotional texture. For others, it was a solitary pursuit, too overwhelming to be shared.

A long time ago, on holiday in rural France, Robin and I took Elizabeth to a *son et lumière* in the nearest town. Amplified music rolled around the square as the facade of the hôtel de ville rippled and billowed with flames, martial banners, fields of sunflowers. Every so often the facade opened, like a book or a doll's house, to reveal dancing and duelling; at other moments, the building fell down and reconfigured itself brick by brick, manifesting in the blink of an eye a drawbridge, towers and crenellations. At the end, when the final firework and chord died away, I caught Elizabeth's expression as the municipal lighting was activated, returning us to drab provincial reality: ramps and fire escapes, swags of netting to keep the pigeons off. That's a little how I feel now.

When he has disappeared into the tube station, I walk on to the bus stop. Rush hour is in full spate. I gaze into the traffic, the flares and clouds of red and gold light swimming before me, and I'm so caught up in my thoughts – worrying away at possibilities like beads on a string – that a bus pulls away before I realise I should be on it. There's a ten-minute wait for the next one so I check in on the items I've listed on eBay. The Paul Smith shirt Robin bought in the sales, too young for him and always on the tight side, has a starting bid and another five watchers. I click through the pictures, appreciating the effectiveness of my careful styling: good lighting, wood hanger, the smooth-ironed placket. A quality item from a smoke-free home.

On the bus, the girl in front is flicking through TikTok at speed: giant omelettes, eyeliner tutorials, the view from the front of a rollercoaster. At Mornington Crescent she switches to Instagram, scrolling fast, liking everything without bothering to look at any of it. I turn my face to the window.

Did they discuss me at all?

Perhaps she said: *Oh God, Ruth Saving is threatening to pop over – we really don't want her showing up! You must remember Ruth? – swotty, massive crush on you, of course.*

Short girl, blonde hair?

No, you're thinking of Jean wotsit. Ruth was... oh, never mind.

Maybe they had that conversation weeks ago. Maybe he said: *I nearly forgot – when you were in Cape Town I met an old classmate of yours at the fundraiser. Ruth something. Spender. No, Saving – Ruth Saving. Are you still in touch?*

Oh, Ruth! She's—

But that's as far as I get. The idea of them discussing me as they lie in bed, the idea of them laughing about me, fills me with horror. It's a terrible thought, though not as terrible as the likelihood that neither of them will have bothered to say my name to the other. There's no need. I'm quite irrelevant.

When I get home I find the monks' box has softened a little in my coat pocket, the damp warping and staining it a little, though the vial of bath oil itself is not damaged. It doesn't matter, anyway. I'm not giving it to anyone. I wanted it for myself. It's only for me.

OTHER PEOPLE'S FUN

* * *

Sookie's social media is a blazing shopwindow over the holidays, and I stand in front of it, appalled and awed by glorious scenes in London and Sussex and Val-d'Isère, where the Inchcapes celebrate the New Year with friends. Murray can be seen from time to time, wearing paper crowns and flying down black runs, and though every picture celebrates his boundless advantages, both physical and financial, I now know that for Sookie these advantages are not enough. I look at him, his expression, and I think: *you don't have a fucking clue.*

Sookie and Jess pick a date for our dinner, and my invitation, when it pops up on my phone, signals that I am an add-on, an afterthought. Sookie doesn't bother to dress it up. *AAGH so hard to find a date, hope this one works for you :)* They will think I'm glad to be included. I suppose I am, among other emotions.

I find myself mentioning the invitation to Jean, as if in passing, when she calls me for the annual catch-up in early January: *oh, this will amuse you, guess who's been in touch?* It is something to say. There is no need to share with her any of the stark realities of my life. When Jean asks after 'the family', I'm cheerful and vague: this is not the moment to fill her in on the departure of my husband, and how my daughter and I got through our first Christmas without him. I will not tell her about the anticipation with which I waited for Elizabeth to arrive home from university, and the recalibration when she slept in until lunchtime and went out every evening. On Boxing Day, she had lunch with Robin at his brother's flat in Kilburn. 'Fine,' she said when I asked how it went. 'It could have been worse.' The raw intimacy that bound us together in the immediate aftermath was falling away, being shaken off. I had hoped for the comfort of comradeship; but in the end we were both alone. Elizabeth is looking forward, not over her shoulder. She wants to be free of both of us: *only natural*, I tell myself. *A healthy sign.*

The firsts are the worst so I'd prepared for Christmas as a warrior prepares for battle, but still there were moments that caught me unawares. The cardboard box containing all the decorations was my undoing, the memories spilling out along with the angels and snowflakes. The sentimental association of each ornament – things Elizabeth made at nursery school, things bought for our first Christmas together, or during a trip to New York – shifted, became tragic. Plugging in the fairy lights, assailed by the familiar glow, I felt the loss all over again. I thought: he has wrecked all this too.

Cards from people who had not heard. Cards that no longer came.

I have learned to be on my guard when looking for pliers or the printer cartridges because there are things lurking at the back of drawers and cupboards, waiting to catch me at a weak moment. I don't mean evidence of his infidelity; Robin is a tidy and fastidious man, not given to sloppiness. He was at pains to leave no clues at the time, so I won't find any now. Instead, there's a breadcrumb trail suggesting his personality: gifts that missed the mark, things he never got around to repairing, gimmicks to fend off the inevitable. A cologne he disliked, broken spectacles, probiotic supplements for the fifty-plus man.

Here is the evidence of those enthusiasms that petered out after a few weeks or months. Late at night, delaying the moment of going to bed, I list these items on eBay:

binoculars, a watercolour set, kombucha jars, the wetsuit he only used twice, which hangs on a hook like a slaughtered seal, filling the cupboard with its rubbery stench. As the radiators leak the last whisper of heat, I bind things in bubble wrap and leave the parcels out on the kitchen table, waiting to be posted off to Warwickshire and Merseyside in the morning.

Once that is done, the cold drives me upstairs. I lie there, Corpse Pose, on what I suppose will always be my side of the bed. I remember the click as he removed his spectacles and put them on the bedside table, just before he turned out his light.

There are sounds from the street: car doors, drunk people shouting threats or laughing uproariously, the yowls of cats and foxes. And then long periods of icy quiet, between faraway calls from the tawny owl who lives in the patch of scrub behind the secondary school.

The flat mutters and sighs to itself as the cold creeps through it.

One night I'm yanked without ceremony into the chill of 4.07 a.m. A noise woke me. Was it outside? On the stairs? I lift my head from the warm pillow and listen, trying to get past the tidal roar of blood. Above the dresser, the oval mirror reflects a ghostly light back over the books, the basket of clean laundry, the silly, uncomfortable button-back chair upon which neither of us ever sat for confessions or confidences.

The bedroom door is ajar – a habit since Elizabeth was a baby – and I can hear someone moving stealthily downstairs.

A floorboard creaks. The bark of a chair leg. A man is opening kitchen drawers, rummaging through my possessions, locating my handbag, my laptop, the box of apostle spoons given to me by Robin's mother the year before she died. He's focused, deliberate, methodical, or he's on something, tense as a trip-wire, desperate for his next fix. *Take what you want*, I think, or pray. *Don't come upstairs. There's nothing up here.* And yet he continues to move around the ground floor, lifting things and assessing them, dropping them into his hold-all. The rooms are raked by the narrow beam of his torch: the rug and sofa, the mantelpiece, the mess of brown envelopes. He stops at the bottom of the stairs and looks up. The beam catches on the banisters, the treads where the carpet has worn thin, the bent leaves of the spider plant.

I know I'm imagining it. My mind is playing tricks, running away with itself. But my terror is so real, a tangible thing, as definite as the dark.

I lower my head and the pillow is cold now. I pull the covers up, dragging the weight over my shoulders to my ears. There's no one downstairs. Silence booms in my head; sleep gets further away. The room watches itself in the oval mirror.

These are the things I do not mention to Jean: the fury and the fear. Instead I talk about Sookie's upcoming supper party, and this reminds her that Clare Snape wants my details. Jean ended up giving her a lift home after the memorial, a village outside Salisbury, not much of a detour, nice to have the company in the car. Clare, who is a GP, emailed the other day, asking if Jean could reintroduce us. Her son is in his final year studying modern languages: he's hoping for some pointers about translation, general careers advice, that kind of thing.

I say I'm not sure how much use I'll be, but by all means, and then she grabs the conversation and tucks it under her arm like a rugby forward, charging off into the customary topics of middle age, which she is constitutionally obliged to make the best of: issues with dogs and boilers, tree surgeons, her father's care home. To show willing I offer the comic anecdote of the slow leak under my kitchen sink, though it doesn't sound very comic in this context, and prompts expressions of concern, rather than the amused recognition of fellow feeling, the comfort of being seen. So this is where we leave it: we wish each other all the best for the new year, and then we hang up.

* * *

Having spent the day toiling over some very dry German, material for a company that manufactures catering equipment, I'm conscious as I get ready of feeling stiff and dull, whatever the opposite of 'sparkling' is. Apart from an engineer in Munich who answered my question about the capacity of a twin-basket fryer, I have not spoken to another human for three days.

A crisp cold night; quiet, as midweek winter evenings tend to be in central London, away from the main drag. At 7.15 p.m. I stand on the wobbly step where they parted, and hear the distorted electronic chime inside, a reminder that this is not her home, just a place where she has been 'camping' for a few months.

I've been wondering whether she'll seem different, altered by her secret or transformed by my knowledge of it, but the old thing happens when she opens the door, the familiar push-me-pull-you of irritation and awe. It's a relief, to feel once again those simple, ancient complications.

I'd forgotten how persuasive it is, her marvellous

self-assurance – every bit as insistent as the ghost smoke of an old cigarette that clings to her hair and clothing. I hand over the expensive bottle I picked out with such care, so she can put it down on a side table and forget about it, and hang my coat among a number of elderly mackintoshes the colour and texture of historical documents.

The narrow hall leads into a reception room, more of a snug than a sitting room. Low-lit and too warm, olive velvet curtains puddling on the carpet, it is filled with the smell of flowers and scented candles. Jess rises, wrapping me in a hug that might be some kind of yoga pose. She holds me there against her tickly mohair jersey for a moment longer than feels completely natural so I'm on the edge of a sneeze. 'So wonderful to see you again,' she says in her new voice, which is deep and melodious, taking its time with every syllable. I can hear she has led many mindful meditations.

The sofa is packed with Kaffe Fassett cushions so there's barely space for one of us, let alone two, though Jess insists there's plenty of room, budging up and thereby drawing attention to how tiny she is. 'How *have* you been?' she asks, clasping my hands between hers. 'Sookie says you're a translator? Amazing, do you work with embassies? The UN? Lots of travel, I suppose.'

'Not exactly,' I say. 'It's pretty dull, ticks over but I'm very low-status,' and Sookie, who has been busying herself with wine and glasses, goes quite still, tilting her head, repeating, 'Low-status?' in a concerned, compassionate voice. I'm aware of the novelty of her full focus. My modest confession has given her a lift, made her feel a little better about herself.

There is the confusion of accepting a drink and I congratulate Jess on the nice mention of FlowYoga in the *Sunday Times Style*. 'Oh wow, it's incredible how many people saw that!' she says, as if she didn't plaster it all over her various platforms. Now she goes through a little humility dumbshow, rolling her eyes and flapping her hands as if her face is on fire, then says she made a new year's resolution to get better about 'boosting' herself. This is something she has had to work at; so – why is this so hard? – she's just going to come out and say it: yes, things are going well. Incredibly well! Not just press coverage, but membership, chatter on the socials – from the right sort of people, too. She and her business partner are in discussions about new outposts in Queen's Park and Clapham, possibly the Cotswold golden triangle and Bruton. Plus, there are a few investors keen to introduce the brand to the Middle and Far East.

'Don't get me wrong; I am so thankful,' she says, as if we've suggested she isn't. 'I accept it's not a fluke – the business is thriving because I put so much of myself into it – but honestly, what with work and the twins, I have to keep reminding myself to practise what I preach. *Remember to breathe.*' She places her palm over her breastbone, closes her eyes, draws air into her nostrils. Her mouth, as she exhales, is set in a flautist's embouchure.

Her eyes pop open and she reaches into her bag for her water bottle. It's this remineralised filtering system she's installed at home, absolute gamechanger. So much more than hydration, really works on energy levels and the immune system. Jeremy is sceptical. He says it makes the tea taste awful. She keeps catching him filling the kettle at the sink!

She waves a hand in disgust: 'Ugh, well, let him have his filthy "brews". Not my problem,' and I remember the anniversary post, *Haven't stopped dancing yet!* and the picture she put up more recently, the two of them in the foyer at the Bridge Theatre (#datenight #happyfriday), the interval at the latest must-see.

We talk about surviving the holidays, or they do; I try to give the impression of fully participating while saying very little. No one cares that I'm quiet. No one notices. This is the way it was when we were girls, and perhaps this is the way it will always be: some people need the light, others shrink from it, preferring the comfort of the shadows.

As they talk, it becomes apparent that Sookie and Jess, the oldest of old friends, are now near-strangers. Common ground is established as they discuss their children. Ava's having her heart broken and is breaking hearts. Finn's on all the first teams. Jess's twins recently went semi-viral with a silly TikTok dance. The mothers' curated grumbles are acceptable forms of boasting.

I look at the paintings and the ornaments while Sookie and Jess find other things they have in common: Sakine's divorce, Jonny Fairweather's breakdown, Fran's daughter who is, frankly, terrible in that new Apple TV series. Every so often I throw little handfuls of kindling on the conversation, politely feeding it with nods and smiles, but this is not my world and they will be aware of that.

In truth I am preoccupied, stuck on the idea – the likelihood, the ghastly probability – that Sookie and Waxham will have sat exactly here, drinking wine, kissing and pawing at each other with increasing fervour, and then somehow their clothes came off and there was no time to get upstairs (maybe he had a ticket for a particular return train, the clock always ticking) so they did it right here, here on this sofa – though because of its size and all the Kaffe Fassett cushions that's unlikely to have been a particular success. But I can't really picture them going at it on the kilim, even though she does so much Pilates. Either way: murmurs and gasps, the sheen of middle-aged endeavour, squelching and so forth. I can barely stand to look at her.

Perhaps it's sublime. Perhaps it's a dreadful mistake. Perhaps it's just something to keep her busy, like volunteering, or an art history course at City Lit. The not-knowing will drive me mad.

'Lovely!' I say, standing up as they stand up, and following them into the kitchen: green and white tiles, mug trees, a family of serrated knives lurching on a magnetic strip. We gather at the pine table, beneath the rattan pendant. Big black letters spelling out '*AL BURRO RISI & BISI*' and '*BUBBLE & SQUEAK*' chase themselves around the rims of the serving dishes, which contain – a bit of a come-down – the usual modish leaves, grains and roots, decanted from Ottolenghi takeaway cartons.

Having persuaded Jess to put aside her special water and have a glass of wine, Sookie invites us to laugh at the decor. We can probably tell, no one has lived here properly for years – well, not even then. Occasionally her parents wonder about selling it, or finding tenants, but they always talk themselves out of it in the end: it's so useful for the theatre, seeing friends, early flights. Obviously, it's a lifesaver for a globetrotting daughter who needs somewhere to crash for a couple of months. So on the whole you put up with the rag-rolling and the mug trees.

We won't have any of it. Oh, we say, but it's just delightful, a time capsule, takes us back – where does the old crockery go, anyway? There are reminiscences, from which I am excluded, about the parties Sookie threw here when she had that funny little gap-year job, folding cashmere in Selfridge's. Sookie's then-boyfriend, an Old Etonian gigging as a Food Hall porter, is now a particularly poisonous backbencher.

When I ask about progress with the house-hunting, Sookie seems taken aback. Oh, I'm way behind, that plan was abandoned months ago. Murray was parachuted into the Singapore office at very short notice – I have a vision of him floating to earth in good tailoring and a silk tie – and the expectation is they'll be based there for the next three years. He made partner on the back of it, the broker found them a fabulous condo in Orchard. Everything's set up. But she can't say she's eager to get out there. The timing isn't great.

Her lovely face becomes sober. Briefly I entertain the notion that she is about to unburden herself, confess they're in difficulties; but that's silly. No, the story is her father hasn't been well and she wants to stick around while he recovers from major surgery. It's something heart-related.

'How's Caroline coping?' asks Jess, topping herself up. Considering the tremendous fuss she made over accepting just one glass, she seems to have developed quite a thirst. I'm reminded of the Commons Speaker being dragged to the chair, a display of showy reluctance.

Caroline – Sookie's mother – is in denial; won't acknowledge that family gatherings and their trip to Corfu might need rescheduling. No, her parents are as bad as each other. Last weekend her father did a three-hour walk and constructed one of his elaborate log stacks.

'Typical,' Sookie says, ripping flatbread. Her mother likes to will things into being. 'Pretend everything's fine, and in all likelihood it will be. Works for her, most of the time, but I'm not convinced it's the right approach when it comes to Daddy's health.'

Jess thinks determined optimism is preferable to catastrophising, her own mother's default setting. Penny had a small role in *Blow-Up* and attended at least three Rolling Stones weddings but now gets panic attacks in the Guildford Waitrose and won't visit them in Chiswick because of knife crime.

Jess's mother-in-law Rosemary, on the other hand. Nothing deters Rosemary; nothing stops her. She's obsessed with Jess's son, Fox. Always has been. Doesn't even pretend to be interested in his twin, Lulu, knocks her over in the rush to get at 'my darling boy'.

Rosemary has major boundary issues. She's nosy and controlling, and Jeremy simply won't acknowledge this, just plays the innocent, as if Jess is making it all up.

'No more, really – oh well, OK, teeny splash.' Jess waits for the bottle to be put down so she gets our full attention again.

When the twins were small, Jess couldn't bear to cut their hair. Fox looked so beautiful, like Tadzio in *Death in Venice*. The long hair was the only thing about Fox that Rosemary didn't like (well, apart from his name); she was forever suggesting he was overdue a Big Boy Haircut, kept saying things like, 'Poor darling wouldn't want anyone to think he's a *girl* – you wouldn't want that, would you, sweetie?' Very unhelpful, given all the stuff Jess was being mindful about (such as trying to avoid rocket ships and fairy princesses and gendered colourways, which meant importing orange starter bikes from Germany at terrific expense).

Her birthday was approaching, and she and Jeremy hatched a plan to take the day off work, have a nice lunch, go to an afternoon screening. It was all lined up, and then the nanny came down with bastard flu. Huge relief when

Rosemary offered to do school pick-up. Jess and Jeremy had a lovely day playing hooky, and when they came home, Rosemary met them at the door, and her eyes, as she called for the twins, were blazing with triumph. Fox ran to greet them, 'and she'd basically scalped him, he was actually bald'.

Jess gives us her best Rosemary: Dame Edna, with a good shake of Blanche duBois. ' "Oh, but you see he begged me, the poor little scrap, he said the other children were making his life a misery – *Cut it off, Gwanny, cut it all off, I don't want to be laughed at anymore* – well, I couldn't refuse!" ' Handfuls of golden curls had been hacked off with kitchen scissors, wrapped in newspaper and thrown in the bin – like fish guts! Terrible scenes. Jeremy poured oil, which of course caught fire. The pale tragic faces of the twins, peering through the banisters.

Fox is now of an age to find his grandmother's favouritism rather oppressive. He jibes when invited à deux to the Natural History Museum, or Fortnum's for a knickerbocker glory. He doesn't want to go, and Rosemary blames Jess for that.

On birthdays and at Christmas, Rosemary is able to express her antipathy to her daughter-in-law through the performative medium of gifts. The presents Jess receives are of a distinctive register, random yet exact. A pack of clothes pegs, a gadget for cutting cling film, too-small leather gloves, a garden kneeler. For the big five-oh Jess was given a waterproof mattress protector. 'How do you thank someone for a waterproof mattress protector? *I'm incontinent with gratitude?*' Every so often there'll be a remaindered cookbook, full of the things Rosemary believes her son and grandson deserve to eat on a regular basis: 'proper meals', joints and pies and casseroles, with pages of steamed puddings at the back. ('Of course Rosemary knows perfectly well we don't eat meat, and are trying to avoid carbs and sugar.') This Christmas, along with a cookery book entitled *Braise Be!*, Jess received a manicure set, one of the emery boards showing signs of use.

'What does Jeremy say?'

'He says I'm being overly sensitive, and his mother doesn't mean any harm, she's a force of nature. He's determined not to get it. To be honest, I've given up looking to him for support on this front.' She laughs a frank and bitter laugh, and then glances around for reassurance, but neither Sookie nor I have our lines ready. There's an uncomfortable pause, and then Sookie says something cloth-eared about counting her blessings, she gets on terribly well with Murray's mother. Jess drinks, and I can see her grappling with the realisation that she has slipped, shown too much sincerity, given herself away. She has departed from the convention of talking in the most general terms about husbands, much as people make jokey small talk about pets. This is no longer a safe topic of conversation.

When she puts down her glass, her eyes fasten on me and I know it's coming, a little lash, to distract from her vulnerability. 'You're very quiet, Ruth,' she says. 'Help me out here. Surely you've got some marital horror stories of your own.'

It feels familiar, the sensation of being picked on by Jess. It has happened before, though I can't remember the specifics. Probably she made fun of my earnestness in class, my earrings, some unguarded remark in the lunch queue. It doesn't matter: I have strategies now. I know I can get her off my case without too much difficulty, and without compromising my privacy, because I do not want Jess – or Sookie, come to that – to know the details of my life.

Breezily I say, 'Oh God, absolutely, I mean, people put up with all kinds of shit, don't they.' Now that my silence has been noted I must say something that will satisfy them, so I tell them about Pavani.

I say she has a job in policy and a husband called Nick, who is a colleague of Robin's. I describe a lunch party Pavani and Nick gave not so long ago, the men gathering on the terrace while we assisted Pavani indoors, because we could see she needed help and that's how we operate; we notice these things; we've been trained to be aware of them, just as the men – even men like Nick and Robin who consider themselves progressive and feminist – have been trained not to notice. I describe putting out the knives and forks, and seeing Nick through the French windows as he stood by the honeysuckle and the apple tree with his back to us, feet apart, nice and relaxed with his stubby green bottle of beer, talking to the men about cricket and politics. I describe Pavani pulling out a stool in order to fetch the extra glasses, and the commotion as she missed the step coming down; the sight of her struggling to sit up, dazed, wincing, trying to laugh it off, murmuring, 'I feel so stupid,' as the broken glass was swept into the dustpan, and someone calling Nick in from the garden, and his air of mild exasperation as he helped her to her feet; how, when one of us mentioned concussion, he was immediately dismissive, prompting Pavani to agree she was *fine, completely fine, nothing to worry about.* His offhandedness seemed carefully judged, as if any show of kindness or concern at that moment might encourage her to make a meal of it. We knew he was itching to get back out there, to the men and the gossip about the new head of department. And, yes, I sound angry when I tell Jess and Sookie about this, because she is a decent woman who deserved better.

He went back outside, I say. She was still pale and shaken, so we persuaded her that a rest would be a good idea. I took her upstairs and helped her onto the bed and pulled a blanket over her, telling her not to worry, we'd take care of everything, one of us would be back to check on her soon.

Darkness filled the room as the curtains were closed. Beneath the window, the men were chatting and chuckling. We heard the snap as a beer bottle was opened, and the chink as the cap fell to the paving. The person on the bed closed her eyes and turned her face away for a private reckoning. She wanted no witnesses but everyone had seen. Everyone knew. Whatever she told herself, everyone knew.

And I remember the women and their expressions, their embarrassment, their sweet solicitous pity, which was almost the worst thing. All the women will have come away with some memory of what happened; but the episode made, I am sure, little impression on the men.

'Did you talk about it with her afterwards?' asks Sookie.

I'd only met her briefly before the lunch, I say, and I haven't seen her since. Not the easiest person to get to know. She's quite reserved, which made the whole thing even worse. I say I sent a thank-you note – a card from the Alice Neel show, if memory serves. But no, I didn't mention it.

'And anyway,' says Jess, 'what would you say? I mean, apart from *I'm sorry your husband's a dick.*'

It might have been different, perhaps, if she had dropped by unexpectedly, asking how I was, and then put her hand on my wrist saying, *No, I mean, how are you really?* She could have rung or sent a WhatsApp, a DM. There are so many ways to make contact.

It is possible it might have cut through if she'd caught me at the right moment. But she sent an Alice Neel postcard, addressed to us both, which she had signed from them both, and this allowed us all to move on as if nothing significant had happened.

Maybe she knew by that point. Maybe Nick had heard department gossip about Robin and the lecturer in medieval magic and astrology, and had passed this on when the invitation came in. Maybe she had agreed to come to the lunch thinking, *this could be interesting*. I remember how it felt, though, her kindness; the novelty of being looked after. The rasp of the wool against my cheek as she pulled the blanket up, the jingle of the curtain rings as darkness filled the room.

We break to clear the plates, and when the fruit and florentines come out the conversation moves to other topics, and it seems there's nothing about my manner or voice that excites any attention. I must appear quite normal to them, even familiar, recognisably the same person – perfectly pleasant if rather shy, perhaps a little awkward – they vaguely remember from long ago. And yet, when I reach for my glass, my hand trembles. It's shock, the shock of the truth, however furtive; the shock of making myself relive that moment and describe it, because in some ways it was one of the very worst moments – the public demonstration of how little he cared – and I never imagined I would speak about it to anyone, let alone Sookie.

It occurs to me (another shock, just as powerful): *I don't miss that. I never have to feel like that again.*

There's that, and that's not nothing.

'Is it OK if I – would you mind terribly?' asks Sookie, opening the window over the sink, applying her cigarette to the tiny flame clicking in her fist. It's a nightmare when she's with the family – sneaking off, hiding it from everyone – but of course that's why she does it. 'I do like having a secret,' she says, breathing out the word with the smoke, and Jess flinches, longing to bat the stink away with her hands. 'I'm so tired of everyone knowing everything about me.' Of course it's a horrid habit, silly and dangerous, a waste of money, but it's good to know you're still capable of shocking yourself. Reassuring, almost. 'This is definitely something I could explore in the pod,' she says to Jess, and I see she's been working up to this, hopeful and jittery. It turns out she emailed Jess a pitch for a podcast called *The Authentic Self*, in which she'll interview wellness celebrities and thought-leaders.

Jess confesses she hasn't had a moment to study the proposal, but it's at the top of her to-do list. She has to say, Sookie's life sounds pretty appealing. Free agent, not answerable to anyone. Jess wouldn't mind a bit of that.

'Right. There are upsides.'

'I get that!' says Jess. She lives for Jeremy's work trips. He's pickier than the twins. Won't touch Thai, aubergine, kale. *Soup's not a meal!* When he's out of town she makes a batch of dal or chickpea curry and sits on the sofa with a spoon, watching *Below Deck*, and it's basically heaven.

She doesn't mean it. However much Jess complains about Jeremy, she can't conceive of a life without him. She's one of those women who needs other people to remind her who she is – to show her herself. She spins through life like a pinball, re-energised by every flipper. It is hard to picture her alone, quiet, sitting still in an empty room. She was always like this. You saw the whites of her eyes as the girls stood up and began to move off at the end of a lesson or lunch break. She feared being left to her own devices because she wasn't sure she had any.

On they go, listing the perks of absence. Being spared the snoring. Sleeping in the middle of the bed. No nose-hair clippers left out on the bathroom counter. Jess begins a long story, something about a conference cancelled while Jeremy was halfway to New Mexico, and my thoughts drift to a memory of Robin otter-faced in the armchair, ankles crossed, green socks, breathing through his mouth, fully and privately absorbed by the small screen in his hand; there in the room with me, and yet not there at all. *I don't miss that*, I think, the memory going through me like electricity. *Living with that was fucking awful.*

Sookie holds the stub of her cigarette under the dribbling tap, then closes the window. She offers herbal tea in a manner that makes it easy to refuse. Jess's long story bored her too. She's had enough of us, of our company and conversation. Perhaps she wants to check her messages. Jess catches the signal and rises to her feet, full of regret: such a drag, meeting with the venture-capital people first thing, she must go home and sober up.

In the riotous carnival of her departure – the retrieval of bags and water bottles, the hugs and kisses, the insistence that we must do this again soon – I find my way back to the kitchen to give them more room, scraping plates and dropping them into the dishwasher. As I dry my hands on the tea towel, preparing to start my own farewell, Sookie returns. 'Just help me finish this,' she says, picking up the bottle. It seems she was only tired of Jess.

'I do love her, but dear God, she brings out the slacker in me,' she says. 'It's envy, of course.'

'You're envious of Jess?'

Sookie props her cheek on her fist. 'Oh, you know – she's so... *busy*. People to see, places to be. All that purpose. Get up and go.' She lets her hand fall to the table, the click of her wedding ring hitting the wood. Then she says, 'I don't suppose she wakes up in the morning wondering what happened to her life.'

Candour, as clear and refreshing as a drink of cold water. This feels like the most honest thing Sookie has ever told me, and I'm filled with a rush of emotions: surprise, sympathy, pity and, yes, a strange kind of excitement, because she chose to say this to me, and her confession at this moment feels like a sort of anointing. Teetering on the brink of an unfathomable future (no longer needed by our children, confronting the thrill and dread of being superfluous), we are both, surely, aware that such gestures of intimacy are rare and bold, full of significance. Not unlike those moments, long ago, when someone you didn't know well waited for you after class, and, as you made your way to the buttery, casually took your arm.

She has entrusted me with something important, and I must honour her bravery, because it will take us somewhere new. It's a turning point. Perhaps before too long she'll tell me about Waxham – 'Ian' – and maybe in return I'll be able to make my own confession, permit myself to be seen. Leaning forward, feeling the warm glow of the pendant lamp on my shoulder, I say, urgently, 'Jess may not feel like that, but plenty of us do. You know? I mean – I do.'

But she does not hear me. She does not react. She keeps talking, as if I haven't said anything; or as if I've said something unremarkable, of no interest. Perhaps it's what I've said; perhaps it's simply that I was the one who said it.

She wonders if she's having these gloomy thoughts because she finds herself here, 'back in London in my parents' flat, on my own, living this funny little life. You know what I've realised? This is the first time in my life that I've lived by myself.' She went from Howard to flatmates to boyfriends to marriage and children, people piling in to keep her company. 'I've never done this before. I'm trying to decide if I like it.'

She yaks away and I lean back, removing myself from the pool of light, saying nothing. There's no point. She isn't listening. She doesn't care what I think. I remember those moments when we've been alone together, in the Witch Wood, in the empty house, and the thought occurs to me: *maybe she really is a monster.*

Sookie continues to talk. Air circulates between her mouth and her lungs, is pumped into words, strings of them, as whimsical and inconsequential as bunting or fairy lights, and while she talks she moves her hands, smoothing her hair or ruffling it, twisting it off her shoulder, and all the time her eyes are on her reflection in the window over the sink. 'My old life seems so far away... and Murray calls me, just to check in, and I see it's him calling, and I've started – this is really bad – I don't always take the call. I'm getting ready to go out, or I'm watching something, and his picture flashes up, and I think: CBA. I mean, I could be in the shower or having an early night. Right? No big deal. But that's not good, is it? I mean, it's not good that I don't feel I have anything to say to him.'

That's not quite true, is it? I think. *You have plenty to say. You just don't want to say it to him.*

'Must be tough for the two of you, being separated like this,' I say, just to be polite.

'No, of course, it's—' and then I see her hesitate, and I wonder if she is on the brink, experiencing the temptation to give this great untold story of hers an airing. On the other hand, it's quite possible she's thinking of something else entirely – something bland and obvious, a remark about visas or Air Miles – in which I will be expected to take just as much of an interest. Who knows? I find I no longer care.

The pause hangs there, a piñata full of potential confidences, but instead of tearing into it with adroit questions, I step back. I offer bland and obvious remarks of my own, conventional reassurances – they'll be reunited before too long, all couples have their ups and downs – that also signal I'm tired and the evening is coming to an end. As I gather my things, I observe her air of faint dejection, and this gives me a blaze of pleasure, an amplification of the pleasure I felt when she told me she was lost in her life.

Cuts both ways, I think, buttoning my coat and making my way out into the frosty night, leaving Sookie behind in those overheated, overstuffed rooms. Perhaps I do have some small power over her, after all.

* * *

I must thank her, of course, but an iMessage will do; no reason, now, to go to the bother of finding a pretty card, stamp and postbox. So I type a few words and press 'send'; and I tell myself it's as if I'm pressing 'send' on her, too, dispatching her in the way that I've been dispatched so many times and by so many people. She won't mind that I've let her go; indeed, she is unlikely to notice. But that's not quite right, because she texts back a few minutes later, a link to a show at Tate Britain mentioned at supper: *Shall I book?* Not responding to this, I feel a tiny dopamine hit, and then I return to the Tyrolean inn website I'm revising for summer visitors, adding details about family-friendly hiking trails, boat trips, geraniums spilling over windowsills.

Perhaps Sookie's more intuitive than I've given her credit for, because she seems to sense my new ambivalence. Maybe she's one of those people who, unused to rejection, finds the novelty of the brush-off quite compelling. Either way, over the next few days I ignore several chatty messages, and decline two FaceTimes. A fortnight passes, another week, and then she's back again, a flurry of activity. I've just opened the door to the estate agent when the first message arrives.

Hey, just checking in, everything OK?

Garrett Wragg is an underpowered young man in a carrot-leg suit, and as he wanders through the rooms he leaves behind him a stickily fragranced haze indicating he didn't have time for a shower this morning. I stand in doorways as Garrett eyes the scuffed skirtings, the place where the shower has leaked, the fault line snaking over Elizabeth's ceiling. Arms folded defensively, I think of the things that happened in these rooms, the moments that dragged or slipped by without anyone noticing, and the moments that changed everything. We were opening tester pots on the landing when I told Robin I was pregnant. I used to feed the baby in that armchair. I was in the kitchen, making risotto, when I understood my marriage was over.

The flat is full of ghosts. They sit on the bottom step learning to tie their shoelaces, they open gas bills, they realise the guy who cleared the gutters nicked fifty quid, they hang up laundry and put out the recycling and write Christmas cards to people they haven't seen for ten, twenty, thirty years. They hunt for thermometers and Sellotape and matching socks and the good vegetable peeler, they go off on holiday and come home again, they celebrate birthdays and exam results and small professional advancements. They do Covid tests and unpack groceries and end their marriages. They have no sense of me at all.

Garrett and I gather at the foot of the double bed, tourists at a tomb. The bedroom faces north, so it's always a little dark; and today, with an overcast sky, it's gloomy despite the lamps. The bed linen, which I shook and smoothed down so carefully first thing, now looks wrinkled and dismal. The pillows were set out like this – one on either side – quite deliberately, to save someone's embarrassment, though I am not sure whose.

Garrett makes a few notes, comments politely on the garden view, and says he's seen enough. As I stoop to turn off the bedside lamp, the thought half forms; and there's the rush and crackle, the white flash, the sense that something is loose and wild in the room. I whip my hand away. The heat fades from the bulb.

These incidents have, I realise, become slightly less regular. After Robin left they seemed to happen every few days; now a month can pass, or two. Today I find I welcome this reminder, because it indicates some household gods will not be appeased or ignored, even as one begins to feel more at home in the middle of the bed, or has cause to remember his feet in those green merino socks. 'Cheap bulb – there's nothing wrong with the wiring,' I say, and this is true; I got an electrician out when it started happening, he had a good look and couldn't find anything – no problems at all.

It's my wiring that is at fault. Over time, the idea has become almost attractive. I think of small stars fizzing and spilling over a tangle of cables, the smell and soot of scorch; something smouldering in the dark, trying to catch fire in a wall cavity or under the stairs. Out of sight, beyond reach.

The phone shivers again in my pocket and I'm filled with resentment. Here she is, still clamouring for my attention. *Are you OK?* really means *Look at me.*

When Garrett has gone, I check her Instagram and see she has put up one of those birthday-tribute carousels, a sequence of Murray cooking half a cow on a gas-fuelled BBQ, riding a Lime Bike, leaping from a rock into a Cambridge-blue sea. In the comments it emerges that he'll be in London next month, just a flying visit, she can't wait. I'll bet. Like Waxham, Murray can't be snooped on as he has no online presence beyond LinkedIn and an inert Facebook.

Sourly I scroll through the curated clutter. Toria Stewart posts a heartfelt RIP to a film star she nannied on a press junket thirty years ago. Dribbler shows off his latest mid-life crisis tattoo (acorns and oak leaves). And here is another dispatch from Jo Upshaw.

Jo is the daughter of my mother's old friend Pam. As my mother has yet to get to grips with Instagram, she insists on referring to *poor Jo* while making a Pity Face, because Pam filled her in on all that business first with IVF and then, later, with custody battles and restraining orders. But Jo seems to be making a decent fist of moving on. Her feed celebrates her 'miraculous, unlooked-for' second marriage and her Grade II-listed mill, with its wildflower meadow and espaliered pears (not to mention the Pigeon Loft, which will launch as a holiday rental next year, along with a range of hand-poured scented candles called things like 'Morning in the Orchard' and 'Walled Garden at Dusk'). Jo is forever bottling sloes, arranging sweet peas, harvesting herbs for simple suppers. In this exquisite atmosphere, the occasional glimpse of her second husband, a bloodstock agent with a penchant for zippered fleeces and pinkie rings, is vaguely traumatic.

It is hard to reconcile this Jo, with her spaniels and stuffed courgette flowers, with the frazzled person I knew long ago, the Jo who tipped oven chips onto baking trays while her boys bullied Elizabeth on the trampoline. Nowadays these boys have buns and beards and careers, and she refers to them as her 'Best Beloveds'. When they visit, they smile uneasily from hammocks and wingback chairs, conscious props.

The world turns, and Jo, freed from a career in arts administration, must go out and document the stirrings of spring in Wiltshire, scattering ellipses like birdseed between Sensitive Thoughts: 'Dusk is sweeping over Flaxton Courtenay as I stand at the Aga, preparing our supper of local chicken with a splash of vermouth, sautéed homegrown spinach and a dish of roast potatoes... Few things are as cheering as the sight of the first emerald-green shoots peeking from the earth; as brave and shy as girls at their first party, they are as irrepressible as hope – each one a miracle, a tender tribute to all that has been, and a promise of all that is to come... A joyful gift, and one I am glad to share with this kind and gentle community...'

She's only giving thanks, I know. She's only counting her blessings. There's no room here for reality, though she will have her share of boiler issues, health scares, financial worries. But Jo's account is an incantation, a prayer, a gratitude fantasy. Surely it's that, rather than a bullhorn fuck-you going out to all the naysayers, the mean girls, the men who never called, the maternity-leave cover who took her job, Simon, and Simon's junior associate who gave birth to their daughter last month; and all those people on the periphery of her life – people like me – whose homes are, unfortunately, not quite as nice as hers.

Sookie tries again, once or twice, and then the messages peter out. She has given up and gone away. Every so often I notice her getting on with her life, the life she chooses to show to the rest of us, and it seems – as I get on with mine – very far away, and even flimsier than my own.

* * *

I've been through a bottleneck with various small but finicky projects, and then the usual happens once I've met the deadlines: brief relief, then my anxieties start to build. What if the work dries up completely? What then?

I have a few days of feeling wretched and then, coming out of the dentist near Russell Square, I learn I've won a contract with a German manufacturer of kitchen appliances, to work on their UK marketing content. The contract isn't worth a great deal, but it's a fillip, something in the diary. It's starting to spit with rain so, buoyed by good news, I decide to take refuge in the British Museum.

I haven't been here for years, not since Elizabeth was small (too small to take an interest, on one of those winter weekends when we all needed to go somewhere for a few hours). At the main gate I'm reminded again of the illustration from an E. Nesbit novel: statuary, swords and storage jars flying between the vast columns into the courtyard, magicked from dusty display cabinets by the Babylonian

Queen. It's a vision that seems less outlandish now, as if, finally, the times have caught up with it.

Inside, the spaces are filled with snaking lines of children in hi-vis bibs, primary-school processionals that carry with them a carnival atmosphere as if en route to a gala event. I go upstairs, where it's quieter. Drifting between glass cases, I am not sure what I'm looking for beyond the shock of connection: something both remote and familiar. A hand gesture, the pleats on a carved tunic, a cat's striped fur on a fragment of pottery. For a moment my attention catches on a display of small sooty-eyed figurines made of stone, clay or blue-glazed faience, but something about their unblinking scrutiny discomfits me, and I move on, drawn to more fabulous and glittering things.

Later, I'm coming home, rising to the surface, stepping off the escalator when I see Gretchen Armitage up ahead in a green coat, waving her Oyster at the gates. I fall back as she crosses the ticket hall but she stops by the exit, daunted by the rain. She checks in her bag for an umbrella and I see the little crumple of her posture as, briefly, she gives in to self-hatred. The rain blows in against her, wetting her sleeve, the skirt of her coat, her boots. She retreats. There's no way around it so I put my hand on her arm and say hello and we laugh and complain about the weather. 'You're more than welcome to share mine!' I say, pressing the button. My umbrella opens with bat-like alacrity. Respecting superstition, I hold it away from us, towards the street; the veil of rain dances before us, coarse and then fine, twisting in the light.

Gretchen weighs it all up: a few moments of enforced intimacy under my brolly versus waiting here, cold and damp, with the *Big Issue* seller.

'Very kind,' she says. 'I only have to get as far as the bus stop,' and we step out together, shoulders and arms bumping in awkward proximity. It is strange to find myself this close to another body.

In a shopping centre the other week, I allowed a sales rep demonstrating ceramic hair tools to use me as a model. I wouldn't have agreed if there was an audience, but the plaza was quiet, apart from soft pop and the splash of fountains, and she looked as if she'd had a lousy day, and I was tired, so I dropped the tote containing printer paper and teabags and sat down on her little stool.

She got to work. I closed my eyes. It was so pleasant: the smell of the product being spritzed over my hair, the click and gentle tug of the hot tongs. Her industry, my passivity. I sat there with my eyes shut and it was, frankly, a wrench when I had to open them and take an interest in her handiwork, the technique she had used, and the discount she was prepared to offer me. 'Thank you very much,' I said, collecting my bags and moving off, away from the fountains and the planters filled with palms. 'I'll think about it, thanks so much—' and I felt terrible, but I also felt, in some way, restored, and that sensation lasted for a while – longer than the beachy waves, at any rate.

Gretchen and I strike out beneath my umbrella and at first we struggle to find a rhythm, each adjusting our step in an effort to accommodate the other, an ancient echo of the three-legged race that our girls took part in during a primary-school sports day. Rain muddles the brake lights in the puddles.

We exchange headlines about our daughters and then Gretchen says she met an old friend of mine recently, at a dinner in Westbourne Grove. 'Sookie Inchcape? When she found out where we lived, she mentioned your name, said you were at Howard at the same time. That place is a very rich resource for Francis and his colleagues at the *Mail*, what with the nepo-babies and Everyone's Invited.' Sookie and her husband Murray – he was at Cambridge with Francis – seem like such a fun couple.

As we head up the hill, water is coursing down it, gushing over kerbs and the pedestrian crossing, creating a lake outside McDonald's. Gretchen says, 'You heard about Sookie's daughter, I suppose. Some difficulty at her boarding school – I gather she was asked to leave. You can't exactly ask *What for?* but it's usually drugs, isn't it? They're looking at those tutorial colleges in South Ken, and Sookie was putting a brave face on it, but for the time being she's cancelled her plans to join Murray in Singapore. Can't be easy. She said she'd had problems getting hold of you recently.'

'I'm terribly fond of Sookie, but you need to be in the right mood,' I say, recklessly. 'She can be a bit one-way, and I haven't had the, um, capacity recently.'

Gretchen makes *I hear you* noises. 'Well, of course.'

'I wasn't sure how close you actually were,' she adds, 'because she didn't know about – *you know*.' Gretchen doesn't want to articulate my difficulty, but I won't help her out. A bus passes too close, sending up a fan of spray and forcing her to raise her voice. '*Robin*. I think I let the cat out of the bag there, she seemed quite taken aback. I hope I didn't put my foot in it.'

I say it's fine, not to worry, I was only waiting for the right moment. As I speak, an itch is spreading along my arms, over my chest, a hateful sensation like scratchy wool against skin, because now Sookie knows something about me that I hadn't wanted to share with her. She and Gretchen have discussed me, pulling melancholy faces, and a little of my power has leaked away as a consequence. Now I understand that flurry of messages: she wanted to show her compassion, her sensitivity, take an interest in my sorry drama, which might somehow make her feel better about her own, both public and clandestine.

But maybe that's too harsh. Maybe she just wanted to find out how I was.

Gretchen says goodbye in a hurry because her bus is sailing towards the stop, a vessel full of warm breath and cold light. She steps on and her bright coat is lost in the jostle.

Along my street, people are coming home with bags-for-life and bicycles and children. Front doors open and close, lights go on and curtains are dragged over flickering TVs and dishevelled sofas, potted plants, floor lamps lurching at barfly angles, many lives underway. For a moment I conceive of this, the vivid cumulative urgency of all these other stories. A life may be small, and still be a part of something frantic and tremendous.

Coming into the flat, I prop the umbrella against the radiator as I get out my phone. Full-length mirror selfie, new jumpsuit. She can't decide whether to stick or twist. *Fabulous!* I type, bathed in the screen's wash of light. *Only you could pull this off.*

* * *

She was so glad when I reappeared. 'I had the feeling it wasn't like you to just *vanish* like that. I worried maybe I'd said the wrong thing – that it was my fault somehow!' She says this with playful frivolity, as if it's the most preposterous idea. After all, it's never her fault.

Her expression turns grave, the shadow of clouds blowing over a pretty view. 'I was terribly upset when Gretchen told me about... you know.'

More squeamishness, more ghastly delicacy: as if my circumstances are unspeakable, as if I might scream or weep or fall fainting to the floor if she used the word 'divorce'. I can't bear – although of course I always do – this particular tone of voice, the expectation I will be ruined by events. She really knows nothing about me. There's that, at least.

'Must have been dreadful for you,' she says. 'I feel so bad you never said anything to me.'

'Oh, I'm sorry,' I say, because it's always all about her. Maybe she catches an inflection in my voice because she lifts her hands and says she's the one who should be apologising.

I say, *There's no need, I'm quite all right. It was a bolt from the blue, a real shock, but that's wearing off now. A relief, really.* It's not clear if I mean the split itself is a relief, or time passing, or not having to talk about it with her. She doesn't press me on it. Either she's being tactful or she isn't paying attention.

It's true that I didn't see it coming. He ran rings around me, upending my belief in my powers of observation, and this – why didn't I see it? – undid me as much as the loss of the rest. However, these are things I don't wish to discuss with Sookie, because there is nothing exceptional about the end of our marriage; it's the usual dreary story. Still, is it such a disgrace, to be gulled by a con? His deceit was so polished; a conjurer's illusion refined, it seems, over many performances.

Sookie will know all about this sort of thing.

She leans against my kitchen counter. I saw her glance around when I let her in, a quick assessment, not unlike the estate agent's. Even as we embraced I could feel her head move as she sized it all up: the cracks in the tiled floor, the shoes kicked higgledy-piggledy under the stairs, the toilet rolls I keep meaning to carry up. She will be wondering what he'd taken, what it was like before.

I can't offer her a G & T because the freezer drawers are stuck, a glacier slab creeping over the ice tray, the bags of peas, Tupperware coffins labelled 'bourguignon' and 'cacciatore' (some of it his handwriting); scraps of dinner parties and festive feasts lost to permafrost. I'm fine without ice but she will feel entitled to it, so I give her the choice of tea or wine, and while I work the corkscrew I tell her as much as I want to, which isn't very much, really. Were she a better listener – keener, more curious – I might weaken, I might be obliged to give her the things she expects: desolation, some kind of confession, maybe some fury, and eventually, as I pull myself together, some brave jokes. But Sookie has never had to solicit friendship. People have always brought it to her, laid it before her, like a gift she has every right to refuse, because of the way she looks and behaves, and this means she lacks some skills that the rest of us consider basic and vital. It doesn't come easily to her, this business of other people's dramas. She has so many of her own.

But still, she's trying. I'll give her that.

'Oh no, how awful,' she says when I mention that the flat is on the market, and I watch her thinking: *What, somewhere smaller and pokier than this?* I'm sure that's what she is thinking.

'I wish you'd said,' she says again. 'You should have told me. I feel so stupid.'

'It was nice not to have to talk about it,' I say. 'To be honest, it was kind of restful,' as if my life is full of clamour and sympathy, people cheering me on for getting up in the morning, sending me Beyoncé memes. 'Sometimes it's good to have a break from it, you know?' and that lands, I can see the flare of comprehension, like a boiler pilot catching. She puts her hand on mine, solitaire winking, a gesture that's meant to be comforting.

'I guess we're in that zone,' she says. 'I mean, it's hard, isn't it? Marriage. I don't know how any of us manage it.'

And just like that, tiring of my story, she shifts the balance of the conversation. Obediently I say of course her own life must be very complicated at the moment, and I ask if she has a date for joining Murray in Singapore. She says, 'Oh dear, well, some news on that front, actually.'

I ask if her father's OK.

That's not the problem, she says. No, he's made a terrific recovery. She popped down to see them last week and he's back to his old self, they did a five-mile walk, his consultant is very pleased with him. No, that's not the reason.

I wait, wondering how frank she'll be.

'Perhaps Gretchen told you, we have a bit of a situation with Ava. Look, sorry – would you mind terribly if I had a fag?' She goes and stands by the open window, tapping the ash over the sill, but after a while she forgets to aim the smoke at the gap. She gives me the encrypted version, which I translate without difficulty: *some problems with her friendship group* means 'allegations of bullying'; *losing focus in class* means 'disruptive'; *grades had started to slip* means 'kicked her out because league tables'. She doesn't hint at drugs but why would she?

'Oh, how awful – poor girl,' I say.

Sookie says it's just as well she was in the country to pick up the pieces. It's completely outrageous, the way the school treated her daughter. My God, and all the promotional guff on the website, wanging on about holistic education and exemplary pastoral care! Such an eye-opener, she feels so stupid for falling for all that nonsense. The place is a meat-grinder, she sees it now. She'll make an official complaint to the governors once things have calmed down. For now, though, she is focusing on Ava, who is settling into her new school, a boutique rescue centre for the delinquent offspring of celebrities.

'We went all around the houses but in the end we decided that keeping her in London was the best option. We thought about taking her out to Singapore, transferring to an international school, but Ava dug in, she begged to stay in London, so much of her social life happens here now… she made a very strong case. So we thought: well, the mews makes it fairly simple, just get her through A levels, and this time next year she'll be all set for art foundation. And then I can join Murray. It's not ideal, for sure, but it's what Ava needs; it's not hard when you look at it that way.'

I picture mother and daughter in the little house, which must feel cramped now, rather than cosy. I wonder where Sookie and Waxham are conducting their trysts.

'Lots on your plate,' I say. 'Poor girl, how traumatic,' and Sookie drifts back to the sofa, clutching her fags and lighter, saying absolutely, careful handling is very much required. Her own role is to administer a steady supply of love and reassurance, confidence-boosting treats, things that make Ava feel good about herself. This reminds her: she pulls out her phone, taps it. 'Just letting her know I'm out – she probably hasn't even noticed.'

I say she is very welcome to stick around for supper, nothing fancy, but she refuses, though she doesn't seem minded to make a move, settling back into the sofa, relieved, perhaps, to share her story with me, if only because no one else is quite so willing to listen. Not for the first time I am reminded how alone she is here, how isolated.

She has established some ground rules for Ava: no going out on school nights, that sort of thing, 'and I'm keeping a close eye on her; you know what it's like, I'm getting whiplash from all the ups and downs. There's this boy Milo, she seems very keen on him, maybe too keen, but I've learned to keep it zipped; anything I say is obviously massively irrelevant and embarrassing – there's quite a lot of slamming of doors going on.' She laughs, but with a certain reverence, impressed by the performative display of teen passion as much as by the emotion itself.

I say, 'Because your advice is worthless, of course! What do you know?' and there's a certain thrill in saying this to her, to her face.

She blinks and says, 'Exactly.' Sometimes she hears this in Ava's voice or catches her expression. It's not even pity. You have to notice someone to pity them, and as far as Ava is concerned Sookie is not really worth noticing. All she knows is that there's something quite pointless about her mother. Something tragically out-dated, like fax machines, or handwriting.

From online surveillance I know that Ava deploys banners, ribbons and black squares in response to various causes and outrages; like her peers, she is quick to identify many varieties of discrimination; and yet she will condemn her mother for the monstrous sin of ageing. I make a little grimace of sympathy, but Sookie's head is bowed. Maybe she's examining the worn patches in the rug; maybe she's admiring her trainers, a brand I recognise from social media (vegan; favoured by the Californian duchess). Or perhaps she's considering the frustrating chaos of her life, the jumble of obligations and blocked desires. My difficulties haven't held her attention for very long.

The song of an unseen blackbird drifts through the window. A supermarket van pulls up close by, the doors slide open and someone starts to stack the grocery crates on the kerb. A toddler is led past, complaining that they are too tired to walk.

'I have no advice,' I say. 'Living with teenagers is a nightmare – I'm still recovering,' a necessary betrayal because in truth Elizabeth was never troublesome, being diligent, self-contained and averse to confrontation, qualities she inherited, perhaps, from both Robin and myself. It occurs to me that the three of us moved through the days like figures in one of those displays you used to see in toyshop windows at Christmas: tiny folk on skates, toboggans and chairlifts, endlessly repeating the same jerky circuits, never colliding with anyone else.

She looks up, meek with gratitude. 'I had all these ideas about how it would be, how much she'd *need* me,' she says. 'But it's not like that. And it's great that we're able to use the mews house, of course... but if I'm honest there's not enough room to swing a cat. And all her emotions are so *enormous*.'

Without thinking, she has pulled out another cigarette, and now she lights it. I say I'll fetch her an ashtray, and as I go into the kitchen I can hear her beginning another routine pantomime of apology: oh, she's so sorry! What a lot of trouble she's causing.

OTHER PEOPLE'S FUN

Locating an unlovely saucer at the back of a cupboard, I remind myself that Sookie has little experience of parenting teenagers. Ava must have gone off to board five or six years ago, and since then someone else has been cooking for her, washing her clothes, waking her up in the morning and turning the lights off at night. Sookie and her daughter were strangers to each other long before Ava sealed herself away behind the chilly disdain of adolescence. After so much sub-contracting, it must be quite a shock, the graft of close-contact parenting.

'It feels rather claustrophobic,' she says, accepting the saucer. 'The thing is, I'd actually started to appreciate living on my own for a change. I rather liked it!' She launches into the speech about how she's never had to do it before: school to flatmates to boyfriends to marriage and children, the same spiel as last time, because she's forgotten I've already heard it. On she goes, the cigarette shrinking and spilling ash, and I suppose if someone was feeling ambivalent about the single life, this little homily about the glories of solitude – *all the time for me* – might boil one's piss.

All in all, this break in the UK is not the end of the world. Murray is OK about it. He has people to look after him (by which she means domestic staff) and a full diary. He'll be over here a fair bit. They'll manage.

I look at her. She shrugs, mashes the cigarette in the saucer. 'Oh, no – he wouldn't.' When Murray was in his teens, you see, his father left the family for a KLM air hostess called Floor. Murray never recovered from that, never really forgave his father, or Floor. He is very easygoing about most things ('mowth thingth'), but that is an absolute no-no.

Murray lives a busy life. He has his career, and that spills over – as is the way with his line of work, with its targets, time zones, client entertaining obligations and corporate memberships – into everything else. It's not so terribly different from boarding school, really. Always something going on.

But is it enough for her? She's not certain. Recently she's noticed a twitchiness, a sense of shortfall.

As she begins to give an account of her situation – which is, after all, only a partial version of one particular truth – her manner is hesitant, semi-reluctant, but before long she becomes more expansive, swept away by the tidal pull of her own drama. Soon she is so deep in her story that she loses track and keeps having to double back to explain something, or provide more context. Her incoherence suggests this story hasn't really been told before: it is quite fresh. I have the sense, as she speaks, of reality shifting. Maybe it's a little like switching between Instagram filters, or adjusting privacy settings from 'public' to 'close friends'.

She knows some couples who thrive on the nomadic life: happy to pitch camp for a while, excited by each new city, and then just as excited to pack up and move on. But for Sookie the process is losing its appeal. It's nothing to do with Murray. He's her best friend, her rock, her champion. He wraps her up in his devotion. As she talks about him, she makes him sound both puppyish and bearish, neither boy nor man. She always knows exactly what he's thinking, no one makes her laugh as much as he does, and the thexth is certainly loads better than the thexth most of her friends seem to be having with their partners of long-standing. No complaints there – none at all. But sometimes she wonders if this – all this – is enough.

OTHER PEOPLE'S FUN

On the one hand, it's so uncomplicated. Everything between them is easy, reliable, safe. Everything just works.

And yet there are times when he seems to know next to nothing about her. He forgets the details: her shoe size, that she dislikes lilies and flavoured gins. His affection is not in doubt, but she wonders if he's paying enough attention. All she wants is to be *seen*. That's fair enough, isn't it? Sometimes there's nothing lonelier than living with another person.

She is telling me this because I'm here and have no connection to the rest of her life and she has forgotten everything about me, because I'm entirely unimportant.

But no: she catches herself, makes an apologetic gesture. 'Oh, listen to me grumbling about Murray, you must think I'm awful. I came here to talk about *you*—' and I make a little sound of protest and deference, and that's enough, she picks up where she left off, complaining about his Christmas present: a Bottega Veneta bag, gorgeous, but almost identical to the one he gave her the year before.

You are a ridiculous person, I think, and just as I have that thought, almost as if she knows I'm having it, she says in a very different sort of voice: 'Oh, Ruth, really, if only you knew.'

I hadn't realised we were so close to the precipice. She takes another cigarette from the packet as she begins her confession, and though her manner is carefully stricken, there's glee in there too. She has to tell somebody.

She's involved with someone. She refers to him as 'Double You', a cloak-and-dagger flourish. They've known each other 'forever'. They had history, some strange electrifying encounters years and years ago. Oh, nothing happened, not exactly. Various reasons. He was married – still is.

'The whole thing wath impothible. But there wath alwayth thomething there. I knew he felt it too.'

Life took them in different directions, they lost contact, years passed. Sookie moved through the set-pieces of adult life, and from continent to continent, and yet the idea of him was always there at the back of her mind. Then, not long ago, their paths crossed again.

This is the point in Sookie's story when I feel closest to her. Here is the thing we have in common. The word 'crush' must once have carried a suggestion of violence, something painful and dangerous, but the meaning has drifted over time. Nowadays, like the cohort known to be susceptible to them, crushes are dismissed as silly and without consequence – not to be taken seriously. But Sookie and I understand their power. They can last a lifetime. Longer than many marriages.

Sookie describes running into Double You again at a *thing* last autumn. She will admit she went along mainly because he was likely to be there. Preparing for the possibility of meeting him again, she'd been pushed into proximity with another half-remembered person: her younger self, whose hopes and fever dreams had little connection to her midlife reality.

When she saw him again on the other side of the room, old feelings came at her with unexpected authority. All these years later she was impressed by the thrilling force of her longing, and also frightened by it.

She was alone, at a loose end, and she was restless. She understood it was an opportunity, one of those rare moments when you get a chance to do something bold and risky. When you're young, these moments happen all the time – weekly, daily – and you assume they're part of life;

but over time they become intermittent, and eventually they peter out altogether. Then you see them happening to your children.

For her younger self, she knew she had to act.

Impulsively, and also with the sense that she had been waiting for a very long time, Sookie scribbled down her number and passed it to Double You, intentions quite clear, no shilly-shallying. When she says this, I remember the fragment of card that fell from Waxham's pocket outside the Wye Building, the corner she perhaps tore from the history teacher's order of service.

So she handed it over, and then she walked away. She had a feeling he would follow up. She'd seen it on his face. Describing the moment when he rang, she gives a small involuntary shiver, and I remember how she moved away from me to take the call, the light filtering through the oak leaves and twinkling on her shoulders and the grass at her feet. He rang, in fact, as the *thing* came to an end, as soon as he could, and that was it: boom. It's crazy. The sex – the *thexth* – is fantastic.

I'm not entirely sure I believe that, but I understand it's an essential part of the story. The sex must be fantastic.

'Oh, Ruth, it's just loads of fun,' she says. 'So exciting, so mad.' Double You had such a hold over her imagination all that time ago, and in the intervening years the idea of him never faded. It became a marker, a reference point. (Of course she hardly knew him back then; not that I can remind her of this. But it's key: because she never knew him, she was free to turn him into whatever she wanted.)

'When did you first meet him?' I ask, and she doesn't blink: around the time she left Howard. She used to call his home number from a payphone and hang up when his wife answered. He never picked up. If he had, perhaps she would have stayed silent, pushing in a succession of ten-pence pieces, listening as he said, 'Hello? Is anyone there?' For the longest time, all boyfriends had to withstand comparison. In fact, one of the first things she noticed about Murray was that he shared Double You's habit of standing in a certain way – hard to explain but it's kind of boyish. It seemed like a sign.

'Have you told "Double You" that?'

'Oh God no, I'm not giving away all my secrets.'

Anyway, he knew they had unfinished business. He doesn't really do social media, 'but he told me he looked me up now and again, just to see what I was up to. He blushed when he told me that – thoe thweet.'

I'm sure it was, I think, imagining Waxham late at night, slack-jawed in front of some boxy old desktop, clicking between infinity pools and pedicures. The blackbird starts up again. I had tasks for this evening: Garrett Wragg has lined up some viewings for next week, and I had planned to put on a podcast and start on Elizabeth's room.

Sookie's face is bright in the wash of late sunshine: she glows with the pleasurable relief of sharing a secret. Then her fingers dart to her mouth. 'Oh, Ruth, this isn't what you need to hear right now... I mean, your own situation... Don't hate me! You don't hate me, do you?'

'Yes – no, of course not,' I say. 'Of course I don't mind, why would I mind? You seem so... so excited, it's nice to see. I'm just surprised. Of course I don't know Murray, but I got the impression from the socials that things were great. It all looked... perfect.'

'Oh, Ruth,' she scolds, 'you can't take any of that seriously. It's a way of staying in touch with people, old friends, family on the other side of the world – pinning down little things, happy moments, before you forget them. But it's not real life. Real life happens somewhere else, everyone knows that.'

When I ask if the thing with Double You is going anywhere, she gives me the side-eye, and I glimpse her as she sees herself: a wild-hearted dashing person, desired and desiring. A buccaneer. 'Oh no, I don't think so. I guess I've been *working through* something. It's a process. That sounds rather brutal but you know what I mean. The thing is, it's fun for now, while I'm here; and then I'll leave London, and that'll be the end of it. He's married, I'm married – nothing's going to change that. No one's going to leave anyone for anyone else. I've been really clear, and he gets it.' Sookie spells it out for me: he's in that little bit deeper than she is. Poor thing, he can't help himself.

I ask if she has done anything like this before, and she says no. 'I mean, of course there are always possibilities, aren't there? Last year, for instance, someone very persuasive came along when Murray was caught up in some work project and I was feeling a bit sorry for myself. He was terribly attractive but a bit of a shit and thank God I worked that out in time. No harm done.'

Sookie and Double You may have history, but that doesn't mean they have any kind of future. She is quite clear about that. 'Now I have this time with him . . . it's fun, definitely a boost, he's absolutely lovely and he's really into me, but it's not as if we have loads in common. Like – it's fine just seeing him every so often, I don't miss him when I'm not with him. I don't share his interests in – I don't know – the Tour de France, or madrigals, or ground-source heat pumps. And that's fine! In fact, it's kind of the point.'

For the time being, this is enough – it's *perfect* – but in the long run she wants more, oh, so much more. She wants more than 'Double You', and it's possible that she might want more than Murray, too. We both know she wants it all. It's what she deserves.

Her father's health scare gave her a crash course in the gorgeous, precarious urgency of life. You don't get a second shot at it, she explains, a TED talk on my Habitat sofa. Now she accepts she has been restless in her marriage for a while. Nothing seismic, they're just drifting. Maybe they'll fix it, maybe they won't.

If she and Murray do end up going their separate ways – and it's far too soon, really, to think about that – the one thing Sookie knows is that by then Double You will be long gone. He may have shown her a way out, but she does not under any circumstances want him waiting by the exit, holding her coat. 'I'll have to scrape him off my plate long before starting any conversation with Murray. If I ever get to that point and he's still hanging around, things could get horribly messy. Dreadful for the children, too. My sister's husband buggered off with some trainee, and my nieces will never forgive him.' That's the most important thing: to protect her relationship with the children. If she leaves Murray, it certainly won't be for someone else. Ava and Finn could not bear that.

The point is, Double You is a symptom, not the cause. When the time comes to fly out to Singapore, she fully expects to leave all thoughts of him at the departure gate. For now, though, he serves a purpose. It's a blast. And it's been so easy, until recently. He's up in London once a week, for research. (She sidesteps specifics, claiming he works 'in academia'.) But now Ava's knocking around, there's no rhyme or reason to her A-level timetable, and suddenly meeting up has become difficult. They've talked about Airbnb and hotels, but Double You isn't exactly rolling in it and Murray pays attention to activity in the various accounts. 'It's really hard, Ruth. I'm struggling a bit.'

'I don't get it,' I say. 'It's not like it's going anywhere – you said so yourself. What's the point?'

'I'm enjoying myself,' she says, 'for a change! Or I was. Just a bit of fun! And now it's impossible, because Ava's always at home, helping herself to my make-up and barging into my room complaining about the wifi. She's always *there*, and I have nowhere else to go.' She blinks at me, her face suddenly doll-like, impassive. Too late, I see I've walked into her trap.

Now I understand what's going on, why she was so keen to re-establish contact. Why she popped by.

She won't, will she? She wouldn't dare. She wants me to offer. Why wouldn't I? No partner, daughter in another city. It would be so easy for me to offer.

I go over to the window and pull down the sash. The shadows are stretching along the street. Looking up at the houses opposite, I find the blackbird, a dot on a chimney pot. Such a small thing, far too small for its song.

She must have other options, other (better, closer) friends. The people she runs and skis with, the people who invite her to sample sales and private views. What about Jess, with her Chiswick conservation-area villa? Although Jess – who can't seem to make up her mind about Sookie's podcast proposal – might dig away at Double You's identity.

Jess aside, there must be any number of BFFs who'd hand over a key with a smirk. But most of them will have children at home, 'other halves', nannies and cleaners, not to mention dog walkers and gardeners.

Perhaps she is reluctant to share this aspect of herself with those friends. Maybe she doesn't actually know them as well as she once did, or their husbands went to school with Murray. It's possible their judgement would feel weightier than mine.

It's a small world, I'm not really part of it, and that's why she's here, looking so desolate, complaining that the thing that was such a laugh, so frivolous and life-enhancing – the thing that was absolutely not meaningful in any way – has been taken away from her. 'I feel a bit flat,' she says. 'I miss it.' It. Not him.

'Mmm, tricky,' I murmur, turning from the window. Her eyes lock onto mine: it's like being jet-washed with woo-woo. *Go on, it would be so easy for you to offer; what'll it cost you anyway, you sad fuck.*

And while it might be enjoyable to punish her by letting the moment pass – playing dumb, offering sympathy but no solution, moving the conversation on to flummeries, and in twenty minutes saying goodbye in the certain knowledge we'll never meet again – I feel myself respond to the power of her will. But there's more to it than that. For all her tiresomeness, or perhaps because of it, I am curious. I wouldn't mind following developments. Why not stay close, witnessing the spectacle at close quarters? I am fairly sure that conflagration is coming, and I want to see who will be burned.

'Oh, wait,' I say, and her eyes light up with confidence, the eyes of a spoiled child who knows all needs will be met because no one can bear to disappoint. 'Wait, I have an idea.'

OTHER PEOPLE'S FUN

* * *

The following Wednesday I go back to the British Museum, because I want to do something purposeful with my exile, and my thoughts keep returning to those massed figurines, with their sooty eyes and air of grave patience.

In Egyptian Death and Afterlife I find them again. As small as chess pieces or as large as shoes, the shabtis stand in rows, heads up, shoulders back, tools in their crossed hands. The information panel states that as servants of the afterlife, shabtis were placed in grand tombs to provide necessary labour in the Field of Reeds. At first the service of a single shabti was considered sufficient for a high priest or a king, but as time passed greater numbers were buried (a shabti for every day of the year, and for every team of ten an overseer in a fancier costume): an army of eternal dogsbodies.

Oh shabti, reads the shabti spell, *if summoned to do any work which has to be done in the realms of the dead, to make arable the fields, to irrigate the land, or to convey sand from east to west, 'Here I am,' you shall say, 'I shall do it.'*

Their black eyes burn as they clutch their hoes, mattocks and seedbags.

Here I am, I shall do it.

Standing before them, regarding them as they regard me, I feel a jolt of connection, of recognition. It's quite overwhelming. While it lasts I do not think about the flat, how I prepared it for Sookie's assignation with Waxham, persuading myself I was killing two birds, doing her a favour but also tidying up for viewings.

Elizabeth's room was already in a process of being abandoned. My room would be out of bounds. *There are limits*, I thought grimly as I scraped stickers from my daughter's bedside table, bagged up old clothes for the textile bank, emptied knickknacks into a shoebox. When I messaged Elizabeth pictures of old treasures found under her bed or squashed at the back of the cupboard, her replies were brisk: *charity shop*, or *just chuck it*. She wants to move on; these items are burrs or even shackles, things to shake off. All the same, I snap an elastic band around the shoebox containing shells and unpaired earrings and flavoured lip balms, and put it aside, along with the toys she loved best: the monkey in dungarees, the felt fox.

I cleared the desk, straightened the set texts and fairytales, dragged the vacuum cleaner around. Then I put fresh sheets on the small IKEA double bed (bought in her GCSE year: so useful for sleepovers) and stood back in the doorway to assess. Sunshine moved in the curtains, Mexican fleabane frothed in the window box, the blue and white pillows lay smooth and plump against the headboard. A pleasant room, if a bit on the small side. Not so long ago, the air in here had seethed with Elizabeth's secrets. Now she was gone, taking them with her. I looked again, and then I shut the door.

Here I am, I shall do it.

The shabtis' steady gaze follows me as I leave the beautiful and terrifying mysteries of Ancient Egypt and pass through galleries dedicated to the totems and litter of other lost civilisations. I'm conscious of their scrutiny as I buy a cup of tea in the Great Court and wander through the gift shop. Perhaps it's this not unenjoyable sense of being seen that means I have no impulse today to filch some silly trinket (a Hokusai fridge magnet, perhaps, or a pair of earrings made of Murano glass), though it wouldn't be difficult.

'We'll be gone by six,' she assured me, and I don't doubt this. They'll leave in good time; she won't want me to spot

OTHER PEOPLE'S FUN

him on the down escalator, or on my street. 'You won't know we were here.'

I wonder if they arranged to meet at the tube station and approached the flat together, making light conversation about train strikes and the weather, unlocking the street door and squeezing past Paul's bike with its curly handlebars, and then falling into my hallway, laughter catching in their throats, finally able to touch each other. Or maybe she arrived at the flat before him and hovered by the bay window, impatient and on edge, greedy for that first glimpse.

There's a hand-tied bouquet on the kitchen table, an arrangement of hyacinths and anemones from a high-end florist. She scribbled a note and tucked it inside the lilac tissue: THANK YOU, DARLING. YOU HAVE NO IDEA. 'Do help yourself to whatever,' I'd said. Two mugs are draining by the sink. The lid is off the tea canister.

The bed linen has been stuffed into the washing machine. Someone went as far as scooping powder into the drawer but forgot to press 'start'.

I can tell from the cushions that no one sat on the sofa. I wonder when they had tea. After.

The bedroom is chilly: someone has raised the lower sash up to the window lock, to air the room. I pull the sash down with a clatter.

Something feels different in the flat. At first I can't put my finger on it but as I drag damp sheets over the airer and snap the creases out of pillowcases I realise I feel lonely. I've never felt lonely here before. Alone, solitary, abandoned, yes; but 'lonely' has sharper edges. It's as if Sookie has left behind her impression of me, along with the hyacinths, just at the moment when I was beginning to find my way in this new life. I feel the pitiful, too-willing presence of this shadow self as the evening passes, an unsettling companion while I watch *Newsnight* and brush my teeth, avoiding my own eyes in the mirror. Sookie has made me feel like this, and I do not like it.

Perhaps she said, *poor old Ruth*.

I wonder if my name will mean anything to him, if he'll remember our encounter at the piano recital, or further back. But that hardly matters now. This is about her; it always is. Her sense that some things are slipping away while other things creep closer. Waxham is not exactly a catch by her standards, and yet I understand that to Sookie their entanglement represents something compelling and significant, a message from the past, a victory of sorts snatched back at the very last minute.

* * *

I hadn't thought beyond the one good turn but for Sookie it was only the start. The day I throw out the hyacinths, their heads lolling on soft and slimy stems, she asks again. She is not anticipating a refusal. 'You don't mind, do you?' she says, and then she keeps talking, excitedly thanking me and telling me what a star I am, a godsend, the best kind of friend, ensuring the opportunity for a hesitant pause is lost. She does not leave space for me, because in her mind I take up so little.

When I come home, I find one bottle of Veuve Cliquot in a gift bag on the kitchen table, another (opened, a glass or two remaining) in the fridge. The times after that she leaves me a jar of Fortnum's blackcurrant curd, a tambourine of champagne truffles.

OTHER PEOPLE'S FUN

One mild spring day I find the garden door left ajar. Sometimes the shower has been used. A towel shoved in the machine, with everything else.

In this way I realise I've been recruited to her adventure. I've become her bag carrier, her accomplice. To reinforce my complicity, she whispers when she rings me, even when Ava's out, and in her whisper I hear relief because her great secret finally has an audience. I know better than to be flattered by her confidences. I serve a purpose. She has no one else. Sharing her secret with me gives it more substance, more crazy authority. After all, if someone wants to be seen, someone else has to watch.

During one of these calls, she mentions an anxiety: he's showing signs of taking it all a bit too seriously.

I make a vague, interested noise.

'No, I mean – of course it's sweet, but I've always been so clear. I thought we were on the same page. Now I'm worried.'

'What happened?'

'Oh, it's just a feeling I'm getting. Things he says – about his life at home, about me. Not good.'

'He's really into you,' I say, and for a moment I feel sorry for him, for his wife, for the mess Sookie could make of it all.

'He's got this idea that he wants to take me away,' she says. 'I mean, ith impothible.' She yawns, luxuriating in his folly, her sang-froid. A pause opens up while she waits for me to ask something.

I refuse to bite. Instead, I say, 'Oh, just a reminder – if by any chance you run into Paul from upstairs, just tell him you're from the estate agents.'

In the digital space, she continues to live her official life of buddha bowls and nature shots in Regent's Park. She is moved by cherry blossom, a BBC drama about domestic abuse, a fundraiser for children with leukaemia.

One in every five posts is a mirror selfie. She has begun to list the provenance of her outfits (a mix of Vinted, Zara and Prêt-à-Porter): a development that suggests she might be trying to launch herself as an influencer.

On International Women's Day she posts a series of old photos, or photos that have achieved bleached edges and sun spots with the help of a filter. Here are her younger selves, alongside other toddlers feeding ducks, little girls in hardhats, teenagers in taffeta or moon boots, new mothers brandishing babies. *Today I've been thinking a lot about the incredible women I'm humbled to call my friends*, she writes. *I'm celebrating the friendships that began at Brownie camp, or during that season in Val-d'Isère (what happens in Dick's Tea Bar stays in Dick's Tea Bar!!) or while waiting to see the emergency paediatrician. Friendship is a superpower, and I am truly blessed to have so many wonderwomen in my life – women I love, whose love lifts me up. Thank you guys!* I recognise quite a few faces. A twentysomething Jess is there, for instance, perched on a stool under a palm roof, sipping a tiki cocktail. (I do not feature. No surprise there. She has never bothered to take my picture. It wouldn't occur to her. I am not that sort of friend.)

Murray is in town and they go to *Madame Butterfly* and Kitty Fisher's.

The next time she calls with that cutesy finger-in-mouth diffidence that means a request is incoming, I say Elizabeth is here for Easter, so no can do, I'm afraid. 'OK,' she says, as if making allowances. 'Fine. Must be lovely to have her home. How long is she staying?'

A couple of weeks, I say, though Elizabeth has made it

clear it's a flying visit. She has coursework deadlines, and then she goes straight into revision, and she finds it easier to focus in the university library. Kindly, she tells me she wishes she could stay for longer, and I almost believe this: she has a new appreciation for the bath, my cooking, and being able to walk around barefoot. Following my clear-out, she could easily unpack her bags but chooses not to, so her room, when I glance into it, looks as it always did, towels and bras and chargers strewn across the bed or over the floor: a transient chaos.

She meets Robin for lunch but doesn't say much about it.

I offer to drive her back to university, imagining an opportunity for intimacy, a few hours in which we will chat and confide in each other, but she falls asleep as soon as we hit the motorway, waking up as we come off at the exit. When I suggest stopping somewhere nice for lunch, she says it might be easier to pick up sandwiches when we do the Big Shop. In the supermarket she chucks shampoo, toilet roll and peanut butter into the trolley while I choose a special-offer Italian red for Clare Snape. It goes into my overnight bag, along with Sookie's fancy chocolates.

As we turn off towards the halls of residence, Elizabeth says, 'No off-roading, OK?' and then she laughs, glancing over to check my response, and I smile back, because it's a brave thing to say and I would not have had the courage to say it, though of course every mile has brought me closer to that other journey, when Robin and I delivered her here, together: our final outing as a family.

Back in the autumn, there were many witnesses, maybe fifty, a hundred. Freshers and their parents waiting anxiously in their cars, unloading, or up in the flats. Today the grounds and reception areas are deserted. A cleaning trolley stands abandoned in the entrance lobby, as if housekeeping has been interrupted by an apocalypse. The smell of mop buckets travels with us as we go up the stairs, past posters promoting club nights, sexual health drop-in and counselling services. The place is silent, apart from our voices and echoing footsteps, the bump and rumble of the suitcase wheels. On the corridor leading to Elizabeth's flat, there's a small movement at the far end as a fire-door slowly swings shut. This evidence of an unseen presence is both a comfort and a little unsettling.

The flat, which looks over bike sheds and a section of dual carriageway towards the blocks of campus, has the air of a ghost ship. Elizabeth wheels her case to her room, with its fairy lights and cactus plants, while I unpack the shopping. I'm assembling our picnic lunch when a girl with a backpack arrives, and after their reunion Elizabeth is stiff and self-conscious with me, caught between homes, worlds, identities. 'I should make a move, I don't want to be late for Clare,' I say, and then I hug her, feeling her awkward affection, and also her longing for me to be gone. 'No need to see me out.'

Back at the car, I realise I feel shaky, almost tearful – low blood sugar – and curse myself for leaving my sandwich. I feel a little better once I've eaten a cheese pasty in a petrol station forecourt while checking Google Maps. When I text Clare my ETA, she replies with a thumbs up.

* * *

It's market day in Clare's village, a practical workaday market, stalls set out around the war memorial, with trays of vegetable seedlings and people digging scoops into sacks of dog biscuits. Clare's house is just a few streets away. As I open the front gate and walk up the path, the clouds pull back and for a moment her little garden fills with hot, vivid sunshine, lime-green flaring in the grass and the jumble of pots by the porch. A dog barks inside, and Clare, her hand on his collar, is opening the blue door: 'Just ignore Hector, he's pretending he hasn't had a walk today; absolute nonsense of course.'

Inside it's cool and dim, beams and low ceilings, the distant smell of burnt toast and old wood fires. Clare moved in four years ago, following her divorce. She used to pass the house every day when the boys were at school, and always liked the look of it. The rooms needed a lick of paint and she put in a new kitchen; nothing major.

The terrier's nails rattle on the flags as we observe the usual rituals – the giving and receiving of chocolates and bottles of wine and cups of tea and slices of cake, the talk of dogs, weather, varieties of rambling roses – while beginning the complex process of assessing one another.

As a girl, Clare was famous for being clever and self-reliant. She was at the edge of things, but it was clear she had chosen to be there, unlike the rest of us, and this gave her a certain cachet. She isn't on social media so I know little about her now, beyond the details (GP, two adult sons) gleaned from Jean as she put us back in touch. *Do pop in next time you're passing*, Clare emailed when she found out where Elizabeth was studying. *Break the journey, stay the night.* Was she pleased or appalled when I took her up on the offer?

Now she thanks me, again, for offering to speak to her son Joe, the student of modern languages who is wondering about a career in translation. She asks if he has contacted me. 'Not yet,' I say, and then I feel obliged to state again that I'm unlikely to be much use to him, as I seem to be stuck in – and here I do my best to strike a jaunty, carefree note – 'the mid-career doldrums'. Clare is stricken he hasn't followed up: *you can lead a horse to water*. Distressed, she pats Hector who scrambles to his feet, an irrepressible swainish hope in his eyes. 'Yes, OK, you win,' she says, rising and putting the milk back in the fridge. I'm welcome to join them for a turn around the village, or I can stay and settle in before supper. I say I'll stay.

The bedroom has sloping ceilings and a view, from the just-open window, into gnarly apple trees. Daffodils in a jug and a collection of summer-holiday paperbacks on the chest of drawers, beneath a faded print of Salisbury Cathedral that no one has looked at closely for years. The cupboard, when I put my jacket away, is stashed with cricket pads, poster tubes and sleeping bags in stubby sleeves.

Once I've heard Clare and Hector depart, I kick off my shoes and lie down on the bed, allowing myself to feel tired, worn out by the drive, the goodbye and the prospect of hours of chat. Overhead, the white paper shade sways a little in the draught. In a neighbouring garden, there's the squeak of a stiff tap turning, the thrum as a watering can is filled. I close my eyes. My breath comes and goes. Maybe, after all, it's rather restful to be somewhere else, free of all responsibilities and associations.

I sleep, and when I wake up it must be from a wonderful dream, because though I can remember none of it I am conscious of the fast-fading bloom of some magnificent happiness, a retreating sense of delight and excitement. I lie there quite still beneath the paper moon, holding on to this sensation for as long as possible.

OTHER PEOPLE'S FUN

* * *

At supper Clare mentions her ex and his new partner, just in passing, as if they're perfectly unexceptional people she doesn't know terribly well. She was walking home from the allotments, she says, with a bag of spinach and rhubarb when she saw someone in the distance and she thought, *that's how Nick will look when he's older.* And it turned out it was him, after all.

I tell her my marriage broke down recently. Clare is sorry to hear that, she had no idea, Jean didn't mention it.

'I didn't tell Jean. I didn't want to. I can't seem to find the words,' I say. 'In any case, it's not much of a story. Most marriages seem to end for the same reasons – quite banal and unremarkable reasons,' and then I find myself describing the journey down with Elizabeth earlier today, and how that brought back memories of the other time we'd made that trip, on a day when there were three of us in the car, and the car – like all the others – was stuffed with duvets, lava lamps and frying pans.

We'd followed the signs and joined the line of Audis and Toyotas snaking towards the accommodation blocks. Even in full sunshine these buildings had the gloomy aspect of prison hulks, and so I'd found myself remarking with too much enthusiasm on the planting scheme and the benches set out between sculpted grassy mounds (which, in truth, reminded me of golf bunkers). Robin had been quiet during the drive from London, but now he cursed the queue, his knuckles white on the steering wheel. There were ten or fifteen cars ahead of us, and we had already missed our allocated drop-off time.

The cars crept forward few feet, and then stopped again.

Robin glanced over the grass towards reception, and then, muttering about this being absolutely ridiculous, he checked the rear-view mirror. Too late I saw what was going to happen. 'What are you doing?' screamed Elizabeth, but he was already jamming his foot down and swinging the wheel, the engine roaring and the car accelerating over the cycle path and the walkway and onto the grass, bouncing up one of the mounds and down the other side, tyres ripping the turf. His face was mottled with fury and other less fathomable emotions.

It is odd, I say to Clare, how all those years of intimacy and shared endeavour can lead to a moment when you realise you hardly know someone at all. At the time, it seemed completely out of character, but perhaps I misunderstood. Perhaps this was the moment when he allowed me to see a long-hidden truth.

Clare has been listening closely, wincing and almost-laughing, and because such attention is a novelty I tell her some more, not a great deal, but as much as I want. When she gets up to fetch the water jug, she puts her hand on my shoulder and gives it a little squeeze.

She pours water into my glass and says, 'It's your story, Ruth, you tell it any way you can.'

Her divorce came through five years ago but she doesn't really know when the marriage began to end. She tells me about the clues she kept missing or excusing, until he lined them up and sent them out to do the can-can for her, because by that point he wanted her to see and force the issue and take decisive action, so he could tell everyone – as indeed he did – that she was the one who told him to leave, that it was all her idea.

To her mind, there's no shame in not thinking to doubt,

never suspecting, never checking phones, bank statements, pockets – behaviours which, Clare understands from friends, are not that unusual, though they come at some cost, surely, to sanity and dignity.

Those last few months, if he came home on time, his car would pull into the drive and he would kill the engine and sit there on his phone for twenty minutes, thirty, and though occasionally he might glance towards the house, where she was starting supper or drawing curtains, there seemed to be nothing furtive to his manner, no particular effort to hide anything. If she asked, he said it was work, and she accepted that, as she did the times when he went AWOL and didn't respond to her calls, because she trusted him and had faith in their relationship. Then it became obvious she was mistaken.

He agreed to go to relationship counselling, and that was helpful, not because the therapist was any good – she was inattentive, and in the quiet moments they could hear her stomach rumbling – but because at that first session Clare could see how little effort he was prepared to make, and so how much he wanted to leave her. This was the point at which she realised it was over. Numb with shock, she let him drive back through the fields and woods as tears soaked her top and dripped onto her lap. Now she understood she knew nothing about him.

They went back to the house, their home, and she found it transformed, the familiar, comforting spaces and objects imbued with horror. She stood in the kitchen with a cup in her hand, and the memory of buying the cup – a weekend in Lewes – was no longer delightful. She began to understand this was how it would be. Perhaps everything would be lost. She did not know.

That evening, conscious of his desperation to be free of her, a wild thing loose in the house, she forced herself to think of practicalities.

Her financial situation was not hopeless, she knew that.

The next task was to make herself conceive of a life without him, an imaginative effort that initially felt impossible, unnatural, beyond her. Doggedly, she applied herself. Like someone telling beads, she forced herself to consider the things she wouldn't miss. His inability to reckon with his childhood, his compulsion to compete with the boys, his drift to the right, his bowel habits. Some time ago he'd made a contemptuous joke about a colleague who travelled to work by bus. Clare had buried that at the time but now she took it out and allowed herself to consider it. Over the months, or years, he must have compiled a similar list of her failings; and the thought of not being inspected for them on a daily basis lifted her a little.

So she thought about life alone, the evenings and weekends and holidays, and to her astonishment it didn't look so bad. *It looked OK*. Almost immediately she could see there might even be some advantages.

The end of this marriage, Clare realised, did not have to be a tragedy for her. From childhood, she had received instruction in how a woman should feel and behave at such a moment. The lesson started with fairytales and pop songs, and continued through to great works of art: a relentless emphasis on the heartbreak, the fear, the shame, the bitterness, and also the guilt (for falling short in various ways, *for not being enough*). But to her amazement, Clare discovered this was not how she felt.

Already that first evening she was freeing herself from the obligation to love him. After all, it would be madness to love – or like, or even particularly care about – someone who could treat her like this, and she was not mad. Her situation was miserable and unanticipated, and it would distress many people, but she began to suspect it would not, after all, break her. Why had she assumed it would?

She went through to the sitting room and told him to leave.

Big things, little things. The week he moved out she bought new bed linen and a vibrator recommended by *Good Housekeeping*, and then she went around gathering up all the things he hadn't bothered to take with him in the great clearing-off (a broken shredder, squash rackets, several Martin Amis hardbacks, a carton of bathroom-cabinet detritus including verruca ointment and indigestion remedies) and put them out by the gate, for him to collect. With every item that she dispatched, she felt her power surging back.

She learned to protect herself. In the early days she was caught out by his status updates, but that was easily sorted: mute, block, unfollow. The words did not do the process justice. It felt tremendous.

Other things had to be reclaimed. The wedding scent, for instance. During their engagement, they'd passed a woman on the street who was wearing the fragrance Clare had been searching for all her life. Clare stopped her and asked for its name, and the next day when he came off shift he went into town and bought her a bottle as a surprise. She wore it for the first time for their wedding, and throughout her marriage the smell evoked the texture of that day, the sun coming out as the car pulled up by the lychgate, the sound of the organ, the raindrops glittering in the yew tree.

For the first few weeks after he'd gone the sight of the fluted bottle with its golden cap frightened her, made her blood run cold. She thought about hiding the bottle in a drawer or offering it to someone – Joe's girlfriend, perhaps. And then one morning she made herself spray a little on her wrist, and as she did so she told herself, as if incanting a spell, *This is mine, I want this back.*

Every day for a week, a fortnight, as if participating in a sacred rite, she removed the cap and anointed her throat, her wrists. Before long, catching tuberose and orange blossom as she adjusted her spectacles or typed a referral letter, she was reminded not of her wretchedness, but of her fierceness, her resolve and, yes, her heroism. The wedding scent had become her battle ensign. It had always given her pleasure, and that now came with powerful new associations. It meant more.

But of course she didn't do it alone. She had support, lots of it. The boys were wonderful. And you can't get through it, can you, without those women in your corner, women who check in on you and book you up for walks and Sunday lunch and cinema trips, women who let you weep when you need to, and tell you you're doing brilliantly because you are putting one foot in front of the other. Friendships hold you up at a time like this, don't they?

Her new life is as full as she wants it to be. It is also peaceful. The sense of tangle and drag – the constant need to consult, cajole and compromise – has fallen away. She had forgotten it was possible to live like this. This is why she has no desire to download an app, create a profile, swipe left or right – although people invested in the concept of coupledom as the natural and superior state will keep asking.

Living with another person can be the loneliest thing in the world, she says.

Sookie once told me much the same thing as she toyed

with the notion of jettisoning both the marriage and the lover, knowing she could do so much better. But her tone was rather different.

I look at Clare, who is pink with the wine and the conversation, sitting at her kitchen table, Radio 3 playing quietly on the smart speaker, light from the kitchen cast over the night-time garden, the brick path and the hunched shrubs. What a pleasant life she has started to live here, with her GP's salary, her settlement, her pension pot. Trying to imagine the orderliness of her finances, I think of one of those antique cutlery canteens, forks and spoons snug in velvet slots, the blades of the knives tilted like rowers' oars.

Like Sookie, Clare will not lie awake at night wondering if she can justify the boiler service and the MOT, if she can in fact afford the car at all. She will not spend her evenings scrolling through barely affordable flats situated over curry houses and within earshot of the North Circular. She will be out with friends, or at choir, or tending to her raised beds, picking spinach.

I murmur something admiring, and she scoffs, suddenly embarrassed. A cello begins to play on the radio, and her expression changes. 'I don't think so,' she says, clicking through to Spotify, and then something occurs to her, something almost amusing, and she says, 'Well, of course – you were there.'

'What do you mean?'

'Fauré's *Sicilienne*. The Founders' Day concert? Oh – so silly, so long ago, you won't remember.'

'Remind me,' I say, but I haven't forgotten: all the parents – crumpled and grass-stained from the day's picnicking, possibly also sunburnt and in some cases quite drunk – entering the New Hall in an unruly procession behind their offhand, embarrassed offspring. Seated on the stage with the rest of the choir, I was glad my parents lived abroad, because Founders' Day, whatever the adults told themselves, was an extravagant adolescent ordeal, a day when we were expected to reconcile the irreconcilable: school and home, friends and family, public and private.

The doors closed behind the final stragglers from the judo display, and then they were thrown open again, to admit the rock star – the most famous Howard parent of our era – plus entourage of mortified child, mortified child's mother (yé-yé singer now running a Provençal donkey sanctuary) and the current girlfriend (a Brazilian supermodel a third his age and twice his height). A master of the late entrance, the priapic icon strutted down the aisle with his earrings and thong necklace, sleeves rolled up on his green jacquard jacket. Everyone pretended to take no notice as he did his celebrated shimmy along a crowded pew towards some vacant seats. Following behind, his daughter looked as though she wished the ground would swallow her whole.

The hall settled into expectancy; the orchestra finished tuning up; someone sneezed. Spangles of dust twinkled in the pink and green light. Jess Carmichael shivered with the effort of stifling a giggle. Then enthusiastic applause as Ian Waxham strode out in a maroon velvet jacket quite unsuited to the heat.

With his hands, he told the choir to rise.

We rose from the gym benches, and before we were ready it was upon us, the timpani, the brass, the great martial alarum that had, during rehearsals, shaken off the taint of high-street aftershave. 'O Fortuna!' we cried. It was impossible not to get carried away. Everyone loved singing this, the squeaky fourteen-year-old boys, the nerds who'd only joined choir because their UCCA forms were short on extracurricular activity, the smokers conscripted as punishment. We sang, and for a moment we forgot ourselves. We were part of something vast and tremendous.

> *O Fortuna*
> *Velut luna*
> *Statu variabilis...*

We raised our voices, and then we dropped them, and as we chanted the violinists plucked away at the strings, redundant bows needling the warm air. The dread excitement mounted. Now I could stare at him frankly, without embarrassment, telling myself he was looking only at me; but because he had selected this piece and everything about him was fascinating, I had done my research (wrestling the relevant volume of the encyclopaedia off the library shelf), so I knew we were singing a lament, railing against monstrous fate and its strange, inscrutable whims. Already, in my heart, I knew better than to believe anything else.

Sweat gleaming at his temples, Waxham held the tension; and then, with a flash of hands and teeth, he shook it free, releasing the strings, the trumpets (not all of whom were exactly in tune), the cymbals, Becky Morris's gong, and the choir, which summoned all its strength for the long final note.

As the sound died away, he lifted his head and showed us his incisors, preparing us for the next movement. It was at this point that I became aware of a disturbance to my left, an agitation, something falling. I saw his expression, and the expressions on the faces behind him, which were turned up to us like a field of sunflowers, as if we were the sun.

Around me members of the choir were backing away or rushing forward. Through the skirmish, I glimpsed the stillness at the heart of it: Sookie Utley lay on the floor, and the people closest to her didn't know whether to touch her or let her be. Her face was quite white, her eyes shut. Waxham came over the stage and bent over her, and he seemed to say something none of us managed to catch, or at least not reliably. He said something and he lifted her with a small grimace of effort, which must have been more to do with the angle than her weight. Her cheek was pressed against his shoulder and her arm fell free, the hand limp and loose. Waxham held her like that, and her limbs and long hair swayed like weeds in water. A fourth-year whispered, 'Is she dead?'

The tenors shuffled back to let Waxham through. As he brushed past, I noticed one of Sookie's bronze ballet flats was coming off, dangling from a toe, and I saw the tiny controlled movement as she twisted her bare foot in an effort to retain it, but the shoe slipped and fell as she was borne away. There was a moment of shock and uncertainty, and then Jess and some others followed Waxham offstage, thrilling to the panic and spectacle. Music stands fell over. Parents got to their feet and sat down. Clasping her mallets, Becky Morris stood at the timpani, disconsolate.

As the deputy head attempted to restore order, I leaned over and picked up the shoe: Capezio, size six, the soft kid interior printed with heel and ball and five little egg-shaped smudges. (Later on, I smuggled it out under my jacket, and when I came to the Humanities fishpond I filled the toe with pebbles and drowned it among the rushes, by the light of the silvery moon.)

People said Sookie was being taken to the san., or to

hospital, that an air ambulance was landing on the Upper Pitch. Someone else said she was in the library, where Miss Carter, the netball teacher, was giving her mouth-to-mouth. Then we were told to calm down and return to our places and Waxham came back with a show-time smile. We rose dutifully to sing the song about fate being bald, but we were no longer in the mood. Perhaps we were worried about Sookie. Or perhaps we felt foolish for forgetting ourselves earlier, allowing the music to ambush us. Now, to show we had never been moved, we smirked and nudged one another and lost our place.

We came to the end, or gave up, and the audience clapped as we sat down. There was no room for the choir elsewhere so we remained onstage, watching Waxham's expression darken as a variety of flutes and violins toiled through Bach and Paganini. No matter how much energy he put into his piano accompaniment, nothing sounded quite right.

Eventually it was Clare's turn. As she arranged her music and swivelled the cello on its endpin, we could see Waxham relax a little. There was a sense that Clare – accomplished, conscientious, well-rehearsed Clare – would turn the thing around. He must have been sure she would be the one to send the parents off into the night reassured that their money was well spent. But when her moment came, it was a disaster.

'Oh, you're too hard on yourself,' I say, but in truth it was ghastly: an early confusion at the page-turn, panic starting to shine on her face, the general awareness that she was out of step with the piano, and this note was off, and so was that one. As Clare's bow dragged and wailed over the strings, some third years began to snicker.

We saw Waxham set his jaw and focus on the finishing line.

When it was over and people began, kindly, to clap, she was already blotchy with tears.

'They say those moments are character-building,' says Clare. 'I thought I'd never get over it, I thought it would haunt me forever – and I was quite right, because here I am, all these years later, rushing to turn it off when it comes on the radio.'

'Bloody Sookie – ruining everything,' I say.

'Poor Sookie,' Clare says. 'It wasn't her fault. She wasn't to blame.'

* * *

How the hell did that happen? Seventeen today. SEVENTEEN!!! Gorgeous girl, you are my sun and my moon. You've taught me so much about love and wonder. I am in awe of your beautiful spirit. Every day with you in my life has been a precious gift. Your creativity inspires me and your courage fills me with hope. Darling, the future is ALL YOURS. I can't wait to see what happens next!!

A baby, a toddler, a little girl, a girl. The last photo in the sequence shows Ava walking down the cobbled mews, away from the photographer, wearing sweatpants and a T-shirt printed with the Doors' 1969 tour dates, an item she probably picked up at Urban Outfitters. You can't see her face but the set of her shoulders suggests she is in a rage about something. I guess this was the only recent picture Ava would allow her mother to use.

Shortly after the post goes up, Sookie rings me and whispers, 'I can't stand it a moment longer – my favourite

N.Peal jersey has been missing for weeks, Ava swore she didn't take it, I had words with the cleaner, she handed in her notice – and of course I've just found it, stinking of weed, full of burn holes, bundled at the back of Ava's cupboard. We're driving each other nuts... and now there's a mini-heatwave on its way. I'm going to run away to my parents' place, do you want to come?'

Her parents' long-delayed Corfu trip is back on and they're keen for her to use the house; it's quite isolated, so they worry less if someone's there, turning the lights on, watering the garden.

I don't want to go away again. I certainly don't want to go away with her. She thinks she's doing me a huge favour. It'll be such a treat for me, I'll be terribly grateful, and then she can cash that in with access to my flat.

I say, 'Unfortunately I can't, I have deadlines,' and she says, 'Come on, I thought this was the whole point of working for yourself – being your own boss. Say yes, Ruth – live a little! You can set up wherever you like, in the study, the drawing room, the garden. It's so peaceful there and I promise I won't bother you. I'm sure you could do with a change of scene. No – I won't take no for an answer.'

'I really can't,' I repeat, and she says, firmly, 'You've been so kind and now I'd like to do something for you.'

How has this happened? Why must she always get what she wants? Why do the rest of us capitulate? I wonder about this, the weakness of my will in contrast to the shining conviction of hers, as I sit beside her in the car, sealed in with her playlist of Fleetwood Mac, Lana del Rey and Mono, and her grumbles about Ava, whose extended birthday celebrations were followed by a similarly protracted hangover.

'Oh my God, though.' Sookie checks I'm up to date on the big news, the fallout from Robbie Shepherd's memoir, the podcast investigation and the subsequent arrest of Norman Chope on charges of historic child abuse. How terrible, Sookie says, poor, poor Robbie. Of course there were always rumours about Chope – well, more than rumours, because everyone called him Norman Grope, didn't they? It was a bit of an open secret – but no one really imagined anything like *this*. Not exactly. The story has blown up because Howard is still a nursery for nepo-babies, kids who almost by accident find themselves fronting Netflix dramas and Marc Jacobs perfume campaigns.

We pass corporate plazas and glassy cliffs of commerce that shimmer in the heat, and then we are funnelled into narrower, dirtier thoroughfares: hipster neighbourhoods specialising in bao and cold brew, which peter out into shabby parades of phone-repair shops and minicab offices. Eventually we reach the point at which the suburbs begin to accumulate, the tangle of flyovers and retail parks, the abandoned roadside semis with boarded-up windows.

It would be polite to ask Sookie about Double You but I feel a stubborn longing not to be polite. It's pointless; all I'm doing is delaying the inevitable. I'm at her mercy for the next few days, and when she gets around to it – there is no doubt she will get around to it – she will have many things to say on the subject, things that perhaps emphasise Double You's ardour and her own chaotic ambivalence, and it will be my duty, as her invited audience, to listen and ask supportive questions and allow her to explore her feelings in luxurious detail. The thought fills me with gloom as we leave the motorway. Now there's a glimpse of the strange, particular line of the Downs beneath milky skies. I say, 'I saw Clare Snape recently. She says hello.'

'Clare, Clare Snape,' she murmurs, changing lanes, adjusting the visor. 'Yes, no, of course. Oh, wait, she was swotty, wasn't she? – good at science.'

'Among other things,' I say, and then, experimentally I add, 'She was very musical,' but Sookie doesn't bite, and of course she was off the premises when Clare flunked the Fauré; it won't have marked her memory at all. Or maybe she has simply resolved to steer clear of any conversations that might lead to Waxham, for fear of revelation, because she has started to feel some unease about their relationship, which was sparked into being long ago by a great imbalance of power. Perhaps it's a secret she is reluctant to share because – no two ways about it – he doesn't come out of it particularly well. Even if, technically, he never crossed a line.

Either way, I find her detachment annoying, and this increases as I outline Clare's pleasant house and purposeful life. Sookie isn't paying attention. Clare wasn't of much interest back then and matters even less now. 'Oh – love this,' she squeals, interrupting me, whacking up the volume: Blondie's upbeat stalker song about following someone through the mall and buying rat poison.

Off the main road, the landscape is marked with catslide roofs, vineyards, a chalk horse. We drive past water meadows and through a village with a tile-hung pub and a sign saying 'Slow toads crossing' and turn down a lane, Sookie pointing out the tall chimneys of the house through the trees. As we come down the drive, I can see it's a farmhouse very much in the Marie Antoinette mode: no cracked concrete or corrugated iron here, no silage smells or wonky gates fastened with blue rope. There are long windows in a flint facade, lavender hedges, a run of stone urns foaming with white hydrangeas. As we step out into the startling heat, I hear a quiet that isn't really quiet at all. The air is full of birds and bees and leaves and the faraway wails of sheep.

The dogs ('silly sausages') are in kennels: Sookie says it's strange to arrive without their noisy welcome.

The door opens to a beeping sound, and Sookie goes off to defuse the security alarm, leaving me to bring in the luggage – my tired hold-all, her shiny roller suitcase, a couple of hessian grocery bags – and gather up the post. The beeps stop. I stack the subscription copy of *World of Interiors* and the Sarah Raven catalogue beside an old blue jug filled with a pretty tangle of poppy seedheads and dried wild carrot. 'Sookie?' I call, but there's no reply so, conscious of trespass, I flip the pages of the visitors' book, scanning messages from people who sign themselves Jinky and Tiggy and Flea. '*Heavenly weekend!*' they write, and '*Sorry M passed out in the dog bed – a tribute to your excellent cellar.*' Somewhere in the house there's the distant clatter of shutters and the shift in pressure as a window is thrown open.

I find her in a long drawing room full of Persian carpets, clothbound books, heavy tassels swinging in crewelwork curtains. A Jacobean chest is loaded with dozens of framed photographs: christenings, weddings, Ava and Finn with their cousins, people at a polo match chatting to Prince Charles.

In design terms, nothing matches, and yet it's unmistakable: the room has assembled itself over time, over generations, with such casual confidence that the contradictions are harmoniously balanced and – though I hate to admit it – entirely seductive.

'What a lovely room,' I say, and she says, as if resuming a

conversation and I'll know exactly what she means, 'He had this silly idea of coming tomorrow but I told him absolutely no way.'

And this annoys me as much as anything, because I resent her assumption that I am just as preoccupied with Waxham as she is – as if her circumstances are uppermost in my mind at all times. 'Who?' I say, smiling, quizzical, waiting a beat. 'Oh, right. Silly me – I meant to ask how that's going.'

I watch her collect herself and decide she can't do this right now. She comes away from the window, making a small, dismissive gesture with her fingers. 'Long story,' she says, moving past. 'It can wait – cup of tea, then you can take your stuff up,' and I'm left alone in the beautiful room with the smell of centuries of fires and the sense I've taken a liberty, been prurient.

Sookie has wrongfooted me; soon I will discover the house has, too. The impression of its rich and slow-accumulated history is an expensive illusion, rather like the amusing trompe l'oeil niches over the staircase, the urns that cast painted shadows. The drawing room, along with the rest – the games room and boot room and five bedrooms and the vast flagged kitchen, shelves arranged with copper pans and venerable serving dishes – is pure stagecraft, the work of the celebrated dealer-decorator Orlando Juckes, who has a little shop in Pimlico and a royal warrant.

Shortly after the house was completed, Juckes gave a tour to a smart interiors magazine. I find the piece online when Sookie has left me in 'Lady Elspeth's Bedroom'. The photographs give the impression that each exquisite room, full of sunlight and flowers, has been captured at the moment when its inhabitants – fascinating people – have strolled away to take an important call, or dress for dinner.

Juckes tells the interviewer about his first visit to the property shortly after its purchase by his unnamed clients (described, in breathless house style, as 'an advertising tycoon and his vivacious and well-connected wife'). Though the house had 'great bones' it had never quite recovered from the 1970s, when it was owned by a legendary music producer, so Juckes's brief was to 'consider the way one space might flow into another, and to find the key decorative pieces that would restore a sense of authentic family life'. Very little is original: the drawing room's marble fireplace came from a Milanese auction house; the pair of crystal basket chandeliers were a lucky find in a Burgundian *brocante*.

I read this seated on the sofa at the foot of Lady Elspeth's half-tester, and when I look up from my screen I notice the ornaments and the furniture selected by Juckes, and the effect of his arrangements: the writing desk in front of the window, the Chinese lamps with their pleated shades. It all looks so easy and comfortable, so attractively improvised.

Coming downstairs a little later, I hear Sookie's voice from the kitchen. I wait by the door, listening, but she's only checking in with her mother, glad the hotel is comfortable, agreeing to deadhead the roses.

It was rude, the way she mentioned him, then dismissed my question. A power move, a flex. She'll be unable to stay off the subject for long: why else am I here? She will always need an audience.

Over a supper of puy lentil salad and bitter leaves, she is a little distracted, her mind elsewhere. She reads me a few messages from Ava, who is displeased to find she has been left with inadequate supplies of avocados. As we finish, there's the sound of Beyoncé and she rises, mouthing, *It's Murray, better take it.* Washing the salad bowl at the kitchen sink, I watch her wandering around on the terrace in the twilight, and I am surprised to see how animated she seems, how closely she listens, and how willing her laughter. When she comes inside, she says she's tired from the drive and wants an early night, she'll see me in the morning.

* * *

I wake early and carry my notebooks and laptop out to the table under the pergola where I spend most of the day, breaking for a scrap lunch and later, when Sookie goes off to the farm shop, a solitary walk along the valley. To my surprise I am fairly productive, as if the semi-performative nature of this work – I'm aware of Sookie moving through the house and garden, occasionally stopping to see what I'm up to – somehow boosts my focus and endeavour. At intervals she appears in running gear or brandishing secateurs or jingling car keys, whispering, 'Don't let me disturb you!' as she passes. Her attitude conveys both respect and mockery, as if it is rather funny to bother with work in this weather, with this view, when she's around.

At mealtimes she chatters away in a manner that is both artless and circumspect. She has the unselfconsciousness that often accompanies charisma; she shows little curiosity, rarely asks me anything, doesn't pay much attention to the things I might say.

She does not mention him again, and this becomes an annoyance. Of course I enjoy not having to ask the usual questions, withholding that courtesy; and yet it's frustrating to be shut out, because I will always want to know more about Sookie's life, so different to my own. Now that it's off limits, I'm more interested in her affair than the things she wants to discuss: the 'Authentic Self' podcast she has pitched to Jess, her sister's ex-husband, the tiresome Ava.

'How are things with you?' she remembers to ask once or twice. 'How are you getting on?' And I give her the benefit of the doubt, telling her a little about Elizabeth, progress with the divorce, the estate agent's incompetence. I am at some pains to make these stories amusing at my own expense – I describe my irritation with Garrett Wragg, and the mad thing that keeps happening with the lamps – but it's not enough to hold her interest. She smiles but her eyes wander and I see her suppressing a yawn, and as soon as is decent she reasserts her dominance, bringing the conversation back to topics she finds more fascinating, those involving herself.

Fuck you, I think, leaning forward and nodding as she speaks, because I'm her prisoner, a hostage in this lovely place until the end of the week, obliged to witness her blithe confidence along with the sun salutations she executes on the lawn first thing (after drinking a cup of hot water with a slice of lemon).

The third morning, she is up early. I'm in the kitchen making coffee when she appears, asking if I'm interested in a swim. It's high tide, which is the best time to go, it's too rocky otherwise, and look at that sky. 'There won't be anyone else there,' she says. 'Weekday morning, we'll have it all to ourselves – we can be there and back in an hour.' I hadn't realised the sea was so close.

Once through the village, the landscape opens up: stony fields and the occasional barn, trees bent into claws along the skyline, a bus stop in the middle of nowhere. The road ends at a visitor centre and a chalet-style tearoom, not yet open. On the far side of the empty car park a crooked line of safety barriers marks off the cliff edge.

To reach the water we climb down a rickety metal staircase, handrails dusty with salt. There isn't much of a beach at the bottom: just a narrow band of shingle being rinsed by a series of ankle-high waves. As Sookie predicted, we are the only people here. The air is still and clear, with the hand-on-heart promise of heat later.

We drop our bags on the stones. While I dig around for sunglasses, Sookie wanders off to take a few pictures: a seagull on driftwood, tufts of sea campion.

Looking towards the lighthouse and the famous suicide spot, I can see fresh white scars where storms and spring tides have torn away chunks of chalk. I'm aware, folding up my clothes, of those great drifts and heaps along the shoreline, the weight of the crumbling wall behind us.

Sookie steps out of her dress and snaps her hair into an elastic. Olive bikini, yoga stomach. 'Shall we?' she says, glancing over at me, and then looking more closely. Too late I remember the sunglasses. I pull them off and tuck them into my bag. 'After you!' I say. She won't be sure. They aren't that distinctive.

The shingle is sharp as knives, the water greenish, clouded with chalk, winter-cold. I stumble in over rocks and through patches of weed. Knees, thighs, arse, stomach, tits, each step an ordeal, my arms finally raised in surrender. At last I'm forced to commit, and there's the shock of the water coursing over my shoulders and neck, smacking my mouth. I swim fast into the swell, moving to stay alive, and within a minute my breath steadies, my body starts to sing. The sun is hot on my face.

The sea lifts me and shows me things – Sookie's tidy progress; a sail on the horizon; hikers on the cliff path – and then hides them again. I swim out after Sookie, thinking of sunlight filtering down towards mussel beds, swaying forests of wracks and kelps, a silvery shadow of tiny fish vanishing into darkness. I imagine the flash of our pale legs as viewed from far below, the signal of our activity, and feel a pulse of panic, an urge to get back to shore.

Sookie bobs towards me. 'The kids don't like the swimming here, they've been spoiled by Abroad, but sometimes I think I prefer this,' she says, and then she tips back and lets herself float, her head lifting and then her toes, the water lapping at her hair, her throat, her arms. I'm reminded of the sway of her body when Waxham picked her up from her swoon, that small twist of the foot.

She talks to the blue sky. The water is in her ears, so it's very much a monologue. She lies there, holding forth while basking, trusting me to listen, just as she trusts the sea's tilting embrace. She describes being out here with her sister and one of her nieces. They were treading water and chatting about this and that when they realised they had become a party of four. A seal had joined them, so close they could see its whiskers.

I am familiar with this story: she wrote it up on Instagram. In ordinary circumstances I would feel obliged to pretend the story is news to me, but she can't see my reaction, so I roll my eyes. *Whatever.*

We are quite far out. No one can see us. No one knows we are here. Anything could happen.

When I look back at the beach, it takes me a moment to locate the marker of our towels. We've drifted a hundred feet to the east. I think of the water around and below me, fathoms of it, black, full of strong, cold currents. 'Sookie,' I say, and then, louder and more urgently, 'Hey, Sookie.'

She rights herself, taps her ears to clear the obstruction, starts to swim back. There's a bit of a pull sometimes, she says, but it's not normally a problem – nothing like the sea off Cape Town, for instance. Still, you have to be careful. When the kids were small she was out here alone, everyone else was picnicking on the shore, and she realised something was wrong, she was being pulled out to sea, steadily, very fast. But she remembered the rules and it was all OK. When she came out of the water, no one was any the wiser.

I say I don't know the rules.

There's only one, really, she says, and that's *don't fight it* – if you feel yourself being dragged out, don't waste your energy trying to swim against it. The current is too strong, you'll get exhausted, that's what kills people. They fight it, and it's hopeless, and they wear themselves out, and then they drown. Save your energy, float, wait for it to spit you out. It'll let you go in the end, and at that point you'll still have the strength to swim back to shore.

To someone else, Clare perhaps, I might say, 'That sounds like the end of my marriage.' But I keep that comment to myself, and take satisfaction in not saying such a thing to Sookie, not wasting it on her.

We are close to the shore now. As my foot touches rock, she mentions Double You. She didn't want to get into it on the first day when the subject came up; she knows she was a bit offish. The thing is – well, she's not sure what's going on there.

She thought things would cool off if they weren't able to meet at the flat. It didn't work out quite like that. Double You wanted to see her anyway, for a cup of tea, a walk.

He suggested the South Bank or the Barbican: public backwaters where they were unlikely to bump into anyone during the afternoon. She had her doubts but things were not easy at the mews, and when the day came, she was glad to have a reason to leave it for a few hours.

To her surprise the encounter was not awkward in the way she had feared. They'd agreed to meet at the Kyoto Garden in Holland Park because the weather was fine, and his manner was old-fashioned and courtly in a way that suited the setting. They walked over little bridges and watched koi carp stirring in the reflections of branches. He was cheerful and amusing, very attentive. Until this point, keen to keep him at arm's length from the rest of her life, she hadn't told him much about her children, 'but I ended up talking about the situation with Ava, and he gave me some advice, very good advice actually', and I think: *I bet he did. An expert in the field of teenage girls.*

Wrapping herself in her towel, Sookie squeezes water from her ponytail. 'I'm a bit freaked out, to be honest, Ruth. I think he's investing too much in this.'

'What do you mean?' I say.

'He's saying some things that are a bit... scary.'

'What kind of things?'

'Just – serious things. About the future. *Our* future.'

'And that's worrying you?'

'Absolutely!' she says. 'The last thing I want is people saying they're falling in love with other people.'

I'm fastening my wristwatch and, standing there in the full glare of the sun, I suddenly feel cold, a little weak and sick. My fingers tremble as I thread the strap through the clasp. The effect of cold water and exercise on an empty stomach, I expect.

'Heavens,' I murmur, putting my water bottle to my mouth, and she shrugs, and perhaps she's reflecting on her enduring irresistibility, her heart going out to him because, really, who can blame him.

The stones clack and roll as we pick our way back towards the steps, and she grabs my arm to steady herself. So yeah, maybe she and Double You are no longer on the same page. 'I was under the impression,' she says, 'that we'd both signed up for this crazy fun thing, which had nothing to do with Real Life. That was the whole point! I thought he got that. But now I'm not so sure.

'He tells me things,' she says. 'And OK, they're nice things, things that no one else is telling me, you know? He says the rest of his life looks so, so...' – she scrunches her nose, summoning up the tribute – 'so flat and neat and colourless. You know: he was half-asleep, and I woke him up. Blah blah blah. He shouldn't say that kind of thing to me, really, should he.'

When she mentioned coming down here for a few days, he said he'd invent a reason so he could join her, just for a night. He had various commitments to rearrange, 'and he made such a song and dance about it, about his *feelings*, how he couldn't wait to spend a whole twenty-four hours with me. I was going along with it and then suddenly I just thought: *Sookie, what the fuck are you playing at?* Because this wasn't meant to happen. So I invited you. He couldn't come if you were here.'

'Why on earth not?' I ask as we reach the steps. This is a difficult question for her, requiring her to switch between realities; she hasn't got her answer ready, and when it comes it's halting, half-lost in the turns as she climbs the tower ahead of me, her ring chiming on the metal handrail, though I catch the familiar line about wanting 'to keep things separate'.

This is the moment when she could have shared his identity with me. But she decides against it, resisting the thrill of revelation, the full confession. She's being discreet. Or possibly she allowed herself, just for a moment, to view the affair as I might: a sad hook-up with a corduroy phantom; a reckless exercise in midlife nostalgia. Held up to the light, there's no doubt the affair might look rather embarrassing – sordid, even. She doesn't want to be associated with something like that. Neither of them comes out of it well.

'That's a pity. He should have come,' I say.

No way, she says.

'Where's the harm? – let him! I'd like to meet him,' I say, wheedling a little, starting to enjoy myself. We've reached the top of the stairs and are standing on the platform, looking down at the expanse of water, the thin line of white drawn again and again on the shingle. 'After all,' I say, 'he's been to my flat, used my mugs – my towels, even!' Sookie looks a bit wan herself now. I feel my strength returning. 'Anyway, you've told me so much about him – I feel like I know him in a funny sort of way.'

'Not so much,' she says hurriedly. 'You don't even know his name.'

'It does seem a bit silly, calling him *Double You*, like we're in some kind of spy drama,' I say cheerfully. 'Go on, tell me. No harm in me knowing his name. Fine, I'll guess. It's William, isn't it? It has to be William. Warren? Wayne!'

We are back at the car now. I know I've wound her up because she dumps her bag in the boot and opens the driver's door without saying anything. By turning him into a comical figure, I humiliate her too. Sookie does not like to be teased.

'Anyway,' I say, sliding into the passenger seat, adjusting my tone, 'I feel for him. And for you. It sounds complicated.' She stays silent as I buckle up.

As she starts the engine, I tell her about my friend Alice who, emerging from the wreckage of a bruising divorce, finally matched with someone plausible on Bumble. This was just before the winter lockdown so, for those first few months, they met like characters in a Jane Austen novel, walking for miles through sleet and gales, never touching, always a metre between them. The more they talked, the more they had in common.

Sookie isn't really listening. She'll only pay attention at the point when she can see how Alice's story connects to her own. So I say, 'All that waiting, that suspense, made it kind of *hot*, Alice said.'

'Right,' she says, perking up. 'I totally get that. The holding off is a massive turn-on. Please tell me the sex was phenomenal in the end.'

I tell her what she wants to hear. In truth, Alice's story ends with a comically dreadful damp-squib shag, and the death of a dream; but this isn't the story Sookie needs today. I don't have a friend called Alice. She's just someone on a podcast I listened to while cleaning the bathroom.

Sookie tries to unravel why the afternoon in the Kyoto Garden gave her pause. Their relationship was founded on little more than impulse and frantic excitement; when she'd first made her move, it felt 'a bit like a dare'. She wanted him because of everything he'd represented to her younger self. Now she can see him – a middle-aged man, whom she describes as thoughtful, sincere, passionate, conflicted

– more clearly. She doesn't particularly want to hurt him. So she's wondering if she should get out now.

I say, 'Oh, wait, Sookie. Hold it right there. OK. Now I see what's going on. It's happening, isn't it?'

'What do you mean?'

'You care about him, too. You're starting to change your mind.'

'I wouldn't say that; I just know him a bit better,' she protests, but I can hear the new uncertainty in her voice, the edge of doubt. Perhaps this possibility only just occurred to her. Perhaps she needed someone else to spell it out.

'Are you quite sure?' I say. 'Because it sounds as if you didn't want him to come because you're scared of your feelings. It sounds as if you're protecting yourself.'

'I'm not!' she says. 'I don't think that's it – not at all.' The car dips down into a deep green lane. A long arm of bramble comes whipping over the windscreen and her hand flies up in front of her face.

'It's textbook,' I say. 'Something changed. You let down your guard, he showed you how he felt, and it freaked you out – because you feel it too. That's why you're in a panic.'

'Rubbish,' she says, but weakly, a query rather than an outright dismissal. I know it has lodged.

Back at the house I return to the shaded table and my German hand mixers, while Sookie disappears to post a photo of a small transparent wave washing over her feet, accompanied by an inspirational quote from Tina Fey ('You can't be that kid standing at the top of the waterslide, overthinking it. You have to go down the chute'). At one o'clock she appears with a plate of tomatoes and burrata: 'Need to keep your strength up,' she says, putting the offering down in front of me.

As the shadows shrink and then stretch, she hovers at a distance, watching me through half-opened windows or screens of leaves. She's there whenever I look up, and I can tell she's eager (or desperate) to explore her dilemma at length and in detail, though of course the story remains incomplete while she withholds the fact of his identity.

It's so confusing, she tells me, whenever she gets the chance. It's such a mess. The stakes are so high and she has to be so careful. She will not jeopardise her children's happiness, her family's equilibrium, for the sake of a whim; well, 'whim' is the wrong word, obviously, because there is such a strong, long-lasting connection. That's undeniable. But as for taking it further? Not a chance.

'What do you want?' I ask, and she sighs and says, 'I don't know, Ruth. I don't know. Oh, I'm in such a muddle.'

It's my final evening, after supper. The light left the sky some time ago and the house behind us is in darkness, but the stone terrace still holds the day's heat so it's warm enough. How pretty she looks, lighting another cigarette, a little flushed and freckled. I understand she needs my support, maybe even my guidance. As her confidante, I have a little responsibility, a little power.

Here I am, I shall do it.

'Maybe it's none of my business,' I say.

'What?'

I say I've been reflecting on the things she's told me about her marriage, and her dissatisfaction with it (though I use the word 'unhappiness' because that sounds better: grander, less peevish, more tragic). I say it is difficult to watch a friend suffer when you are powerless to help. I hesitate at this point. It's necessary to hesitate. I have her full attention now, and it's an exciting sensation. I can feel how eager she is to hear what I have to say next, how avid. People always long to be told their own stories, shown their true selves.

'Perhaps I shouldn't say this, Sookie – forgive me, but it's been on my mind, it seems important. You've been so honest with me. I guess I feel I should be honest in return.'

I say there's a change in her, a mood shift, whenever she mentions Double You. When she talks about him, I glimpse a different Sookie: lighter, brighter. I say this person reminds me a little of the old Sookie, the one we all knew at Howard.

I take a breath, summoning up my courage, or giving that impression. 'This might be out of line,' I say, 'but I get the feeling you haven't been happy, *really* happy, for a long time.'

It's a critical moment. Anything could happen now: she could burst into tears; she could tell me to fuck off. But I have nothing to lose so I press on. 'You deserve to be happy, you of all people. You're *made* for happiness. Someone needs to say that to you.'

I can see the whites of her eyes in the gloaming. She's very still, processing my little speech. The tip of her cigarette glows and fades. She's thinking.

She says, 'Wow. OK, I wasn't aware it was coming over quite like that. Maybe I exaggerated a little when I described the situation with Murray.'

'Maybe. Oh God, I'm sorry. I shouldn't have said anything.'

'I wasn't aware of expressing myself quite in those terms.'

'Not in so many words,' I say. 'No, of course. My mistake! I got the wrong end of the stick when you said he'd stopped noticing you. Forget I said it. None of my business.' And then I let the silence develop. It spreads and thickens around us with the dusk, binding us closer together.

'I mean, of course Murray and I have our ups and downs,' she says. 'After twenty years, who hasn't? We've got through worse. No, I wouldn't say I'm *unhappy* with him. Not exactly.'

'Of course not,' I say.

'This thing... my secret: it's just a distraction, really – a way of killing time. You see, Ruth, it doesn't have to *mean* anything,' she says, and there's a patronising edge to her voice, as if I'm being rather unsophisticated.

Beyond the lawn and the trees, there's a noise from the dark fields, a scream, an owl, Sookie says, or a fox. She shivers and we begin to collect glasses and dishes from the table. She goes ahead of me, holding the French windows wide so I can bring in the tray. All the lights are off in the drawing room. I can't see a thing. 'Hang on,' she says. I hear the sound as her fingers brush over surfaces, locating the lamp cord and feeling along it for the button.

The flash – the burst of carnival brilliance – is a shock, and yet not a shock. Like the opening of a pop-up picture book, everything springs up and away from its shadow: ornaments, fire tools, patterned cushions and her hand, with its platinum ring, in the act of reaching. Then the bulb dies and the light vanishes, taking the tableau with it. Only the print on a cushion remains, an impression of ovals floating in the dark for a moment or two.

* * *

Sookie drives me to the station the following morning. Given the weather, she has decided to stay on a little longer: Ava is going to a drum-and-bass event this weekend (her boyfriend scored passes as he's doing shifts on an empanada truck) so there's no need to rush back. As she pulls up outside the ticket office, there is still a residue of last night's froideur in her manner, a slight reserve. Perhaps that's why she didn't ask me to sign the visitors' book, underneath the dashing scrawls of Jinky and Tiggy. Or perhaps she was worried we'd miss the train.

She pops the boot and I grab my bag. It's another warm morning and the baskets of petunias and lobelia hanging beneath the eaves are dripping water, which pools along the kerb. I blink into the sun, not sure of her expression. 'I'm sorry if I said the wrong things last night,' I say. 'I think I put my foot in it. I didn't mean to make it worse.'

'Oh, forget it,' she says. 'It's my mess, I'll sort it out. Don't worry about me.' She glances back towards the road, and says, 'Look, would you mind if I make a run for it? If I'm quick, I might beat the barriers.'

Once she's gone, I dig in my bag for the sunglasses. Walking through the ticket hall, I catch my grainy image on an overhead CCTV screen: the glasses aren't very me, if I'm honest, but maybe that's the point. They allow me a new perspective. That person up on the screen interests me. She's someone with quite different concerns and expectations; someone who simply cannot waste time at a level crossing.

Sookie does not reply to my thank-you text, and her social media gives nothing away. Her various accounts stay dark for a week, ten days, and then crackle back into life: a selfie with her colourist, Finn taking a wicket against Charterhouse in the final match of the school year. The mixture as before. I don't interact with any of her posts. My strong instinct, now, is not to interfere in any way. She has to work this out on her own.

OTHER PEOPLE'S FUN

* * *

This time last year – there's no point in having these thoughts, but they come anyway. Technology makes it worse. On his birthday, the heartless algorithm presents me with a photo slideshow ('Robin Over the Years') set to coffee-shop acoustic. One picture fades into the next: the Brecon Beacons, various Christmases, a nap on the sofa. I took so many pictures of him and in all of them he now appears a stranger, full of mysteries. Was he unhappy here, sitting on a grassy bank, handing Elizabeth a sandwich? Or here, sipping an aperitif in the Venetian sunshine? I will never know, and that uncertainty leaves a mark on every other part of our history: the moments when I believed myself to be safe, understood, at peace; the moments when I knew him to be a good and honest man and was proud of him. Was I wrong about all of that, too?

But there is progress. I no longer lie in bed at night going over events, pulling the details apart, searching for answers; and waking in the morning, I'm spared the ordeal of remembering it all over again. Somehow, I've begun to accommodate my grief. It is no longer a distinct and separate entity, a fact I must endlessly and painfully re-encounter; it has become part of me, a thing I have somehow taken on board, and in this way I am being liberated from it and also (I suppose) from my marriage, that repository for – it now seems to me – so much magical thinking. If the task is close to impossible, there is perhaps no particular shame in failure.

Sookie labours under a different kind of marital illusion. She is dissatisfied because she feels entitled to so much more. More event, more sensation, more feeling – whatever the cost. Who can blame her for that? Robin wouldn't, that's for sure.

The final shot in the sequence is the most recent picture of Robin – the last I took of him. There he lies, otter-faced in the armchair, ankles crossed, green socks, eyes fixed on his phone. Click, swipe, refresh. There, but not really there. He's all packed up and tomorrow, as arranged, he will make his escape – taking his bags and boxes, his suit carrier and his case of drill bits, the gadget for making espresso – to his brother's flat, where for decency's sake he will camp for a few months between his trips to Basel, before telling me about Hannah and moving in with her.

Lying there, he's unaware that I'm watching him through the doorway. He looks quite at ease.

I still don't understand the impulse that made me take this photograph. Perhaps I wanted something I could scour for evidence once he was gone. Perhaps I wanted to remember him at his most absent. Perhaps I wanted one last piece of him. Oh, I don't really know. But I took my phone from my pocket and composed the shot – I remember trying to fit in the angle of his feet, in those green merino socks that my parents had given him for Christmas – and then I pressed the button. I thought my phone was set to silent but I was wrong. At the shutter click, his head went up like a gundog's. 'The fuck are you doing?' he said. I didn't have an answer. I went away without saying anything.

Ending the Robin slideshow, I check on Elizabeth, who is backpacking around the Cyclades with friends whose faces I have come to recognise, even if I don't know their names. She hasn't updated her Instagram for a few days and the most recent picture is still the girl with pink hair against the bougainvillea. I wonder whether Elizabeth's hiding her posts from me, to stop me worrying about sunburn and spiked drinks and drugs.

Mindlessly, I start to scroll. Now the rest of it comes at me with the usual force: other people's fun, their hobby-horses and bêtes noires, the hills on which they are willing to strike a warrior pose, if not actually to die. Trans spats, seabass *en papillote*, that particular shot of the Grand Canal from the Accademia bridge. Dribbler has lost two stone, thanks to portion control, an achievement he marks with a koi tattoo. Jo Upshaw brandishes yet another smug trug – sweet peas, courgettes and broad beans – while wibbling on about the simple joys. Following her triumph at the International Booker, my erstwhile professional rival Fiona Hennessy plugs her event at the Cheltenham Literary Festival. I lose fifteen minutes on this crap, and then I snap out of it and check the items I'm selling online.

On the local Facebook Marketplace, Francis Armitage has made an offer for Robin's never-used bike panniers, which I found under the stairs, beyond the string mop and the collapsible clothes airer that wouldn't stop collapsing. His bid falls short of the RRP sticker but it's the only one and is accompanied by a friendly message asking if he can collect in a couple of weeks, when he and Gretchen are back from holiday. *Fine*, I type, and then, cravenly, I add a smiley. As I press send, my phone shivers, receiving a message from Sookie.

She needs something. She always needs something. Perhaps I need something too.

* * *

In the afternoon, I look around several properties in keeping with my new circumstances. A sobering experience, though in each place I try to find something to be positive about, remarking on the storage space, the natural light, even (when completely desperate) the number of power sockets in the living room. It's important to keep Andy and Khalid and Orla sweet, to show them my appreciation, because there's a chance something better will come on their books, and if that happens, I need them to think of me, the nice sad lady.

I stand in kitchens that people have attempted to jazz up with money plants and clip-frame art, bedrooms overlooking recycling hubs or delivery bays, and to my terror it's not a stretch to imagine myself here, unpacking the shopping, watching TV. 'I'll have to think about it,' I say to Andy and Khalid and Orla as we step out into the street. 'I'll let you know.'

Sookie told me they'd be long gone by six but as I let myself into the flat I hear, over the whine of the spin cycle, a cupboard door banging shut, and this fills me with weary rage because it doesn't matter how much I give her, she'll always take just a little bit more. Key still in the lock, I wonder whether to slip away again, give her another half-hour, but she must have been listening out because she comes to greet me. 'It's only me,' she says. 'I thought I'd hang around until you got back. You don't mind, do you? You don't have plans?'

There's a strange interlude while she ushers me into my kitchen and digs around in my fridge to retrieve a bottle of Whispering Angel, her gift, which she opens while making solicitous noises: 'You look like you could do with a drink – here you go.' At this moment, the flat feels more hers than mine. I'm so tired of her, of this, her bag on the counter, her jacket over the back of a chair. Everything's upside-down, back to front.

The spin cycle ends and she declares an ambition to hang everything out on the line: such a warm evening, it'll dry in a flash. I'm not so sure but, obediently, I follow her into the garden, tipping the leaves off the plastic chairs, telling her a little about the flat-hunting. She asks some questions and provides the appropriate responses, but her mind is elsewhere.

Sounds hang in the warm still air between the houses: the sounds of my neighbours preparing meals, catching up on the news, kicking balls against walls, over and over, thud, thud, thud. At the end of the tussocky lawn, the sunshine has reached the clothes line where Sookie pegs pillowcases next to the forlorn bunting I put out earlier: a pair of jeans and a couple of tops, a nightdress, a bath sheet, several National Trust tea towels, a week's worth of Primark knickers.

'Do you ever wonder how we got here?' Sookie asks, and it's a signal that she's listened long enough, and now it's her turn to speak.

So, on Thursday, Ava goes off with the empanada truck to a drum-and-bass festival near Godalming. The following morning, Sookie is prepping for a meeting with Jess (hoping finally to get her to sign off the 'Authentic Self' pod proposal) when the call comes through: Ava's using a friend's phone because hers got nicked; she's fallen out with the boyfriend; without Apple Pay she can't buy food or a train ticket. Sookie cancels the meeting and jumps in the car, 'and when I arrive she's dehydrated and hungover and God knows what else. I knew I had to get her to eat something. We weren't far from Crowfield, and I thought of the Cartwheel. You must remember the Cartwheel? Hot chocolate with swirls of aerosol cream on top, doorstep toast, everyone smoking like mad. The manageress used to ding a bell if a teacher came in. It's still there! It does flat whites now, and smashed avo with dukkah.' It's not clear if that makes her happy or sad.

Sitting in the Cartwheel, watching her daughter eat shakshuka, Sookie is overwhelmed by melancholy. 'Because of course it doesn't seem so long ago that I was seventeen – that we were,' she corrects herself, drawing me in. It's a cheap trick, but at least she bothered. 'Like an idiot I said that to Ava, "It seems like yesterday," and the *look on her face*... as if I'd used the wrong pronoun or defended J. K. Rowling. Silly, I know, but yes, it hurt. I'd dropped everything for her, and still I'm unbearable, a total cringe, just as my mother was when I was Ava's age. I always assumed I would be a different kind of mother. But here we are.'

Poor Sookie, so used to affirmation she'll even expect it from a teenager. I lean towards her, my chair rocking a little on the uneven paving, murmuring soothing things.

'Oh, you are sweet, Ruth,' she says. 'You're such a good friend. I feel bad about it – you've got your own problems, and here I am, dragging you into mine.' She looks at me, and she might be thinking: *sad Ruth with her sorry little existence, no wonder she takes an interest*. 'The things you know about me!' she says. 'You know all my secrets.'

'Not all,' I say.

'Every secret worth knowing. You're the only one.'

'Ah, but that's not quite true, is it, I don't even know

his name,' I say, the cue for her complacent pleasure as she brings me up to date with Double You.

She's incredibly grateful for today. She wanted to see 'him', of course, but she also longed to escape the mews for a few hours. Murray is in town, working out of the Bishopsgate office before they head off to Italy; Finn's home from school, sleeping and eating and bathing at all the wrong times, burning through milk and toilet roll at a ridiculous rate. And as discussed, it's heavy going with Ava. The mews house is too small, it's back-to-back catering and tantrums, Sookie can't get a moment to herself.

'What did you tell them you were doing this afternoon?'

'I said my old schoolfriend Ruth was a bit low because of her nasty divorce, and I was going round to cheer her up – take her out of herself for a bit. That's what friends are for, right? Poor old Ruth! No, really, I'm just happy I can help.' I laugh, because we're pretending it's a joke.

Anyway. Double You. She can't remember the state of play the last time we spoke.

I say, 'Well, you seemed to be . . . having a bit of a wobble.'

'That's right. I was. And then I started to think about something you'd said.'

Sookie asks if I remember how she hurried off after dropping me at the station. Now she explains Double You was on his way to the farmhouse, responding to a message she'd sent late the night before, after our conversation on the terrace. I think of her lying in bed with her doubts, composing her message, pressing 'send', and then I think of him waking at 4 a.m. for a piss or a private reckoning, and reading her message in the darkness as Carla slept beside him.

I wonder how Sookie phrased it. Perhaps her message said, *We need to talk* or *I can't do this anymore* or *What was I thinking? I can't live without you.*

I also wonder what he told Carla as he threw things into his little rucksack in the morning, but I can guess. I am familiar with the things women are told at these times. The point is, as I was returning to the flat – putting milk in the fridge, opening windows – some great reunion was taking place, a drama worthy of those marvellous rooms. After the cramped proportions of the mews cottage or – even worse – my place, Waxham must have enjoyed the contrast. Thanks to Google Street View I've had a look at the estate house assigned to the director of music. A quarter of a mile from the school campus, it has a blocky postwar aesthetic and a rotary airer listing on the lawn. I imagine Waxham standing, as I did, in the drawing room, and being really quite unprepared for the strength of his feelings.

Sookie says he stayed for twenty-four hours, the last gasp of the heatwave. Whenever she attempted to raise pragmatic concerns about their future, he was ready for her, so ardently persuasive that she 'sort of gave up'. Nothing felt quite real to her, and when he left she felt sick with uncertainty, somewhat dazed by his conviction. It dawned on her then that he truly wanted a different sort of future and was prepared to do all kinds of damage to achieve it, upending the lives of her children, and Murray, as well as the lives of his wife and daughters, like a drunk flipping tables in a saloon.

She goes over it with me. Maybe he's right and what they have is rare and precious (all the more so because it was lost for many years, and has come back to them at a point when so many things are being shuttered off) – but what if it isn't? Perhaps this adventure has been built on a misapprehension, a distortion, an echo of something that didn't happen a long time ago. How is she to know?

As she havers, he's talking about fresh starts and second chances and how they owe it to themselves to act decisively; the subterfuge is becoming unbearable, and he thinks his wife has some suspicions. He asks her to decide, one way or the other.

Sookie has tried to sound a cautionary note, flag up her unease, but it doesn't really land. He's so *full on*, so *emotional*. And as she says this, it's plain that despite the mess and the risk, or possibly because of it, his ultimatum delights her. It makes her feel vividly, thrillingly present; for the first time in decades she can steer the plot, instead of being propelled by it.

Something has been pushing her to the side of her own life. He has rescued her from the margins, restored her to the centre of her existence. It feels good.

'Look at you – you're all lit up,' I say, and it's not a lie; it's the truth, a truth that in turn has its own effect, so she glows with its significance and magical authority. I'm the only witness to her adventures, and naturally she will listen to what I have to say, because I'm an old friend who has her best interests at heart.

Still, she shakes her head, murmurs a protest.

'It seems to suit you,' I say. 'Because you're bloody *radiant*.'

'It's no good,' she says. 'It's going nowhere – it can't. It's hopeless. I must let him go.'

Let him go. It's the language of stagecoaches and heiresses, duelling and moonlight. I think of him in his kagoule, his little backpack slung over one shoulder as he stumped off to the tube.

I say, 'Are you seriously telling me you're going to end it?'

She leans forward, knocks fag ash into a spidery bush. 'Honestly, Ruth, it's impossible. You don't know the half of it.'

I raise my eyebrows, daring her. 'Tell me.'

'I can't,' she says, but after a beat of hesitation, a concession: for the first time she acknowledges the possibility.

'You can,' I wheedle, and she considers me through the smoke, assessing the moment. So close. Nearly there.

She's thinking: *where's the harm in telling Ruth the truth?* She has been so careful and discreet for so long, and it's nearly finished, and this way she could wring a little more drama out of it, and I would understand, because I'm familiar with the Waxham legend, such as it was. But there's something else. Perhaps she needs me to be shocked. I may well find the enterprise – not the infidelity, which is entirely run-of-the-mill, but the middle-aged hook-up with a teacher – a bit icky and problematic. (One can't bear to imagine what her children, well versed in the politics of power and consent, would say, were they to find out.) My disapproval may be the push she needs to finally extricate herself, to hop back into her safe and comfortable old life. Just a silly episode. No harm done.

Her protests are weakening. She taps her cigarette again, but there's no ash. Just nerves.

Here I am. I shall do it.

'For God's sake, tell me,' I repeat, and this time I sound slightly exasperated, as if I might be losing interest.

When she says his name, I make my eyes huge and round,

and my mouth opens into an O so I resemble the emoji. 'Wait, wait!' I say. 'What? Say that again.' She repeats it, the ugly name which is so lacking in glamour of any kind, and then she starts to laugh with embarrassment and relief – it's *crazy*, she's *crazy*, the whole thing is *insane* – and I join in, and then we're both almost crying and gasping for breath. It's the sort of laughter you only share with a really good friend.

Eventually, when she can, she tells me how it started. How she went to the memorial at Howard wondering if he'd be there, still curious, and, as they met and talked, felt herself being caught up again in the old madness, even though this person was rather milder and more genial than the spectre who'd haunted her since adolescence. How she dared herself to slip him her number, because *why not*. How he'd called while we walked to the car. She describes that moment, listening to his voice as she stood beneath the oak tree, and how it wasn't necessarily about him: it was about feeling a sudden connection to her younger self, as if she had been given the chance to put something right, avenge something. 'Well, you know the rest,' Sookie says. 'And now he tells me his marriage is over, they're simply coexisting, he doesn't want that old life anymore, he wants *me*.'

'OK – wow,' I say. 'I was not expecting this. *Ian Waxham?*' And then we start to laugh again. 'When you told me about Double You, you said you had "history". I mean, of course we all *wondered* at the time,' I say, when I've collected myself.

'Oh, that. It's terribly innocent, really. It wasn't just me, was it? Everyone was mad about him! He was older, but he wasn't *old*; he had that sensitive-poet thing going on. Come off it, Ruth. I bet you had a crush on him too. Admit it.'

This stings like an insult. It's an intimate joke at my expense, a joke she has no right to make. 'No,' I say sharply. 'To be quite honest, I never really saw the point.'

She pulls a 'yeah, right' face. I wait. Someone is calling a child for bathtime. The sun moves in the trees. A plane draws a thread through the sky. 'In some ways it seems so long ago,' she says dreamily, 'and yet it feels so fresh. I can remember all the little details: what I was wearing, how hot it was in the New Hall.'

'The Founders' Day concert, when you passed out,' I say. 'Or did you? We wondered at the time if it was all a bit of a put-on to get his attention.'

Tit for tat. She doesn't like that. It was a boiling day, she'd had too much champagne at lunch, the New Hall was stuffy. She remembers feeling sick and dizzy, and everything rushing at her and going black, then she 'came round' backstage.

She describes the sensation of proximity, the damp heat of the performance coming off his body, the smell of him; it was overwhelming. At this point her only reference points were Toby Everden and those grotty boys at the Gatecrasher balls. But this: this she wanted. She was weak and overwrought, it had been a long day – and yet she found it in herself, as he lowered her into a chair, to do what she longed to do. She put a hand to his cheek and pressed her mouth to the edge of his.

It was the thing she'd dreamed of for months and months, 'we'd all dreamed of it, and in a way it felt like I was doing it for *all of us* – I can't believe I had the nerve, but I was past caring by that point – I wanted to see what he'd do.'

He turned his head away and as he settled her on the chair he said, kindly but firmly, 'That never happened,' and then people were pushing into the wings and swarming around them: her friends, other teachers, her parents.

'Who did you tell?' I ask. 'Because everyone was talking about it,' and she says no one really, she was absolutely mortified.

'No one really?'

'Somehow Jess knew. I may have dressed it up a bit, given her the idea that he'd maybe initiated it – to make myself feel better. You know what girls are like. She was furious with me. We were booked to go interrailing and she sulked all the way to Amsterdam.'

So nothing really happened, and yet it did, all this time later. She and Ian have revisited that moment, comparing their versions, neither of which will be completely reliable.

At the time he didn't take the incident seriously, certainly not seriously enough to report it either to colleagues or his wife. He was aware he had 'a bit of a following' and such things were not unknown. Sookie was leaving Howard in a matter of days and there was no need to add to her embarrassment.

But the episode will have stayed with him because – as we all understood at the time – Sookie was the stand-out star of our year. She was not the brightest, or even the prettiest, but everyone believed she would go on to have the most interesting life because of her marvellous self-assurance, a mysterious and compelling quality that the rest of us mostly lacked. So, yes, he was flattered. He admits he thought of her from time to time, looking out for her name in the *Bulletin*, casually happening upon her social media every so often.

'Must have been good for his ego,' I say.

'Right.'

She sits back, smoke drifting through her fingers into the dusty leaves.

'That's it, that's the whole story,' she says. 'It's crazy. *I'm* crazy! What do you make of it? Be honest. You won't tell me anything I don't already know.'

I lift my hands in a gesture of helplessness, and impatiently she says: 'Go on! Tell me this only happened because I was at a loose end, tell me it would destroy the kids if they found out, tell me I'm married to a decent man who doesn't deserve any of this. Go on, Ruth, say it, say it, say there's no bloody future with Ian Waxham,' and then she can't help it, she giggles again, gassed to be sharing this wild, hilarious secret with someone who can truly appreciate it. '*Ian Waxham*, for God's sake! He's on statins, his last holiday was a lecture cruise of the Norwegian fjords! Honestly, what am I doing?' The laughter runs out at the same time as her cigarette, which she flicks into the shrubbery, heedless of fire. In a smaller voice, she says, 'Tell me I'm making an idiot of myself, Ruth, tell me to stop.'

I could do that. But is it what she needs to hear? Would it be fair? Mightn't it be a fine thing, to watch her break free, leaving all bridges blazing behind her? I conjure it: various terrible scenes and then the two of them setting up shop in Shepherd's Bush or Battersea – her new life will be less comfortable than her current one, for sure, but not *that* much – where the sitting room will have to accommodate Waxham's piano, his collection of sheet music. He's not far off retirement, and the school will push him out early, keen to move on and refresh the music department following the fallout of the Groper Chope scandal. Ava and Finn will refuse to see her; shocked friends will keep their distance. It'll be just the pair of them, together at last, discovering all the things they have, and don't have, in common.

I say, 'Is it a mistake? You keep saying that, but how do you know?'

I am only asking her to examine her assumptions and impulses. Her throat moves as she swallows. 'Of course it's a mistake,' she says, but without force: she is distracted, wondering if she is missing something. 'There's *no way*. I mean, ith impothible.'

'Is it, though? I mean, after all this time – that has to mean something. Doesn't it?'

I see her allowing herself to think about this properly, then shying away from it.

'I couldn't do that to them,' she says, and I say, 'Forget about them, for a change. It's always about *them*, isn't it? What about you? What's right for you? What do you think you deserve?'

She blinks, thrilled by the question, the reminder of her assiduous sacrifice. She won't deny Ian has been good for her: not just the sex, but the validation, the excitement and (OK) the sense of jeopardy.

While the flat was out-of-bounds they met once at the National Theatre (quiet in the afternoon, also dramatically underlit and handy for his train). They were standing in the foyer when a group came down from the restaurant, and among them was Dribbler, you know, whatsisname from school. She and Ian made a run for it. Dribbler was unlikely to have spotted them, but still. The adrenalin was wild. Like a bungee jump.

She hasn't felt like this for years – but what does that count for, exactly? It's just a matter of endorphins. At moments she's convinced by their relationship; at other times it seems little more than an elaborate in-joke she's having with herself. They're such different people! Today, for instance. When Ian arrived, he held out his headphones and clamped them over her head so he could play her some music, Bach or something, and she had to stand there (in my kitchen) smiling, as if she understood what she was hearing, as if it meant something to her, when in fact she simply felt embarrassed, self-conscious, bored. That was all! And he waited, watching her expectantly, a soppy expression on his face, sure of his gift.

'I've been over this with my therapist,' she says, 'and I understand why this thing happened, at this particular moment. I was a little lonely, and without the usual obligations – and I wanted to know *if I still could.*' She throws up her hands, scandalised by her recklessness, yet enchanted by it too. 'Poor Ian,' she murmurs, as if she pities him for being susceptible to her piratical spirit, as if he never really had a chance. 'Poor old Ian! With his walking poles, and his dental emergencies... oh God, I wish I could tell Jess. She was so mad about him. I'd love to see the look on her face,' and as she says this I'm reminded of those faraway girls, the length of their shadows in the late afternoon.

She holds out her glass for another splash. The lights are going on in the houses, yellow and white rectangles through the branches. Perhaps people are looking down, watching us: two friends gossiping, making the most of a fine summer evening. 'Tell me what to do,' she says again, languorously, as if she's spoiled for choice.

I say, 'Don't ask me. You don't need my advice.'

'Oh, but I do,' she says, and perhaps she means it. 'I do value your opinion. I've been holding onto this secret for so long, and it feels so good to let someone else in – makes it seem more real somehow.' A performance always needs an audience.

I string it out for a little longer, going through a ritual of reluctance, because it's not my place and what do I know and I don't want to speak out of turn; and then, because she insists, I weaken.

Presenting my argument, I'm very hesitant and delicate, and this gives me authority. It's important I remind her of her worth, her potential, the years ahead of her. As mothers, as women of a certain age, we are not meant to put our own needs first or consider the things we might be entitled to, though the men around us do this all the time. I say I've noticed her growing in confidence over the last year, and that has been good to see; because when we met at the memorial, she struck me as lost, rather defeated.

This makes her tip forward in her chair. 'Was that really how I came across?' she asks, and I can see this has rattled her; she thought she was on top form at the memorial.

I say that when we went to the Witch Wood I sensed her sadness, her lack of confidence, and I recognised it because at the time I had my own secret. Robin had just left me, and I was feeling wretched and uncertain, and couldn't bring myself to share this with anyone. 'I didn't know then exactly what you were sad about, but it felt familiar, somehow,' I say.

She opens her mouth, to ask a question or raise an objection, but this time – unlike the evening in the country – the momentum is with me, bearing me forward like the tide, so I press on. 'I felt for you – I really did. The more you told me about your life, the flimsier it seemed. It's not enough for you, is it? Something's missing. That's why it seems a bit... glib to dismiss this thing you have with Mr – Ian. Seems to me, it happened for a reason.'

'You think?' she asks uneasily. The idea is disturbing, but perhaps also attractive, because she is beginning to understand it might offer her some dignity, after all. She wasn't expecting dignity.

'That's the question I keep coming back to: I can't work out why you're so determined not to take it – him – seriously.'

'Oh,' she says, shifting in the plastic chair. 'But it's not really about Ian, is it? I've unpacked this with my therapist. Things just... lined up. You know. Where I am in life. Murray on another continent. Kids busy with their thing. Perfect storm. Doesn't have to mean more than that.'

'Oh, come off it,' I say. 'You can fool your therapist but you're not fooling me.'

'I'm sorry?'

Here I am, I shall do it. 'You have feelings for Ian Waxham,' I say. 'He can see it. I can see it. But for whatever reason you can't bring yourself to acknowledge it. And I wouldn't say anything, Sookie – I tried not to; of course, it's none of my business – but it's such a waste! You've got this chance, this person has come back to you half a lifetime later, and he's in love with you... Are you really going to throw it all away?'

'I'm not in love with him, Ruth,' she says, smiling. It's wan, but it's a smile, rather a graceless smile at that, because I'm going out of my way here, I'm showing her something that might make all the difference to her life, if only she'd accept it.

The half-light between the houses is turning a little chilly, dampness creeping over the grass. I stand up and stretch, perhaps because I am stiff, or perhaps because I am fed up, and then I begin to pick through the largest of the dried-out pots set out along the path, tugging out ground elder, herb robert, sticky spines of goosegrass. My movements might be construed as irritable. 'Seems to me you have a choice,' I say over my shoulder, throwing a handful of ghost-white roots on the paving. 'You can pretend none of this matters, and go back to the life you have with Murray, which sounds awfully easy and comfortable. Or you can face up to it.'

'Look, Ruth,' she says, 'I appreciate your thoughts, but I'm not sure—'

'You're right, I shouldn't be saying any of this,' I say, straightening up. 'I'm sorry. You've been so open with me, you don't have anyone else to talk to, I was only being supportive – I didn't mean to overstep the mark.' At the garden tap I rinse the sticky sap off my fingers and then I rub my hands together, to dry them: a gesture that reminds me, distantly, of mattocks and seed bags.

She has been listening to me attentively – it's always pleasant to bask in someone's full and generous attention, even if they are telling you uncomfortable things – but before she can respond we are startled by music: hand claps, beeps and clicks, the bravura sass of 'Single Ladies'. She looks down at her phone and says she'd better get this. As I walk towards the washing line, I can hear her advising someone to check the tumble-dryer, it's bound to be in there.

The bed linen is still a little damp but I won't risk leaving it out overnight. Unpegging items, folding them under my arm, I'm conscious of her finishing the call, drifting towards me. As she approaches, I say, 'Of course I have no right to say any of this to you. But this feels awfully close to the bone, you see, because I've spent the last year picking over this stuff, wondering why I was prepared to put my own needs aside for so long. Why didn't I ask for more? Why didn't I feel entitled to do that? And I've come to see my expectations were too high to start with – and then later, they were too low. So yes, please, do think about what you deserve. That's what I mean.'

She's watching me doubtfully, but then her gaze shifts sideways, over my shoulder and up into the trees, and in that moment of dreamy reflection I can see the idea taking hold, catching fire. This is how it starts. She is allowing herself to imagine a future with Ian Waxham. When she turns to me, her eyes are brimming with tears. 'My life is such a mess,' she says. 'I don't know what I want.'

'That's not true,' I say, quite gently. Maybe this is the moment when I should go to her and take her hand, reassuring her that I believe in her and am sure she'll make the right choice, but I can't, because my arms are full of damp laundry, and she is making no effort to help me with it. So I simply say, 'You do know, Sookie. Seems to me you've always known.'

* * *

Francis stands on the doorstep in cycle clips, office shirt open at the neck, face blotchy with exertion. He has started cycling to work as part of a fitness drive: it's OK going in but the uphill slog at the end of the day is a bastard. He refuses tea, but wouldn't say no to a glass of cold water.

Leaving his bike lolling cosily against Paul's in the hallway, he follows me into the flat and through to the kitchen, and inspects Robin's panniers while I fill a glass at the sink. When I turn around, he's studying Waxham's flyer for the bursary recital, still tethered to the fridge. 'I'd forgotten you were there with Sookie. I was at the same college as her husband, Murray.'

As it happens, he's in the process of commissioning a piece about another Howardian: scholarship boy Mono, hotly tipped for the Mercury Prize and now an op-ed sensation after breaking off from his Glastonbury set to denounce the government's stance on music education – though Francis concedes *Mail* readers are less interested in his politics than his relationship with Piper Haste, the American pop princess. Francis really wants to find someone who knew Mono at Howard. That kind of background colour always lifts a piece.

'I'll ask around,' I lie, 'but he was long after my time, I'm afraid.'

A few nights later, Mono is a guest on *Newsnight*. He sits there in a beanie and the gold-framed glasses favoured by Seventies' serial killers, arguing that the government is committing social vandalism by slashing educational funding for the creative arts. When Victoria Derbyshire mentions the expensive education he received at a fancy boarding school with a theatre, recording studio and 'wellness hub', he acknowledges the 'insane privilege' of his full scholarship. He will always be thankful for it, he says, because it gave him access to an extraordinary music teacher called Ian Waxham 'who asked a lot of me, but gave far more in return'. It's a disgrace, he says, that such teaching, with its potential to change lives, is withheld from most kids.

In early September, Clare, visiting London for her son's graduation, invites me to tea at her Bloomsbury hotel, 'so Joe can pick your brains!' Joe, crammed into a club chair in the hotel conservatory, a tiny cup in his ham-like fist, finds the meeting excruciating: I can see his life flashing before his eyes as I tell him about my work for the German manufacturer of kitchen gadgets. We are all relieved when he slopes off to have a pint with a mate.

While the waiter whisks away the evidence of his presence, Clare checks her phone, encountering a message that prompts a self-conscious, rather performative smile, so I'm obliged to raise an eyebrow. Bashfully she says she has started seeing someone: a civil engineer from Bath, divorced, two adult daughters. Early days, who knows, so far so good.

'I didn't know you were out there,' I say, and she says the practice nurse gave her a pep talk and helped her to set up an account. It's nice to have someone to do things with, she says, and remembering how complete her life had seemed to me in the spring, how she seemed to have achieved a state worth navigating towards, I feel a little let down, even betrayed. 'Why don't you give it a whirl?' she asks, and I say, 'Oh no, I'm not there yet,' as if I intend to be one day, as if we can agree that aspiring to be part of another couple is proof of recovery, of resilience and mental stability.

The truth is, I don't want anyone else cluttering up my life. Now I have it all to myself, I have started to appreciate the space, the quiet, the marvellous lack of drag. Sometimes it comes back to me, the effort involved in coupledom, the strategies and patience and cunning necessary for the most banal of tasks: replacing a kitchen tap, say, or deciding what film to see at the cinema. I can't imagine going back to all that lock-step business, the suggestions, the debating and counter-arguments, and finally saying yes to the wrong thing, just to get it over with.

Clare wonders if I've been following the Mono hullaballoo. She belongs to one of the Old Howardian Facebook groups, don't hate her; she keeps trying to leave but the tech won't let her – it's like Hotel California. The admins are people I vaguely remember, some of whom moved back to Crowfield so their own children could attend as day pupils, and because they've drunk all the Kool-Aid they maintain the page as a vibrant propaganda outlet. That's where Clare saw the *Newsnight* clip: an impressive young man! If only Joe had some of that drive.

'Nice mention for Ian Waxham,' I say, and she asks if I saw *The One Show*'s follow-up, reuniting Mono (beamed in mid-tour) with 'the teacher who changed my life'. Clare thought Waxham looked rather wrung out. Not surprising, really.

According to the Facebook group, Waxham's wife booted him out recently. There was quite a scene in the driveway and the neighbours ended up calling the police. He's involved with someone else, apparently. Well, aren't they always? As she speaks I have a sense of an arrow shower, somewhere becoming rain.

Leaving the hotel, I stop on the steps and dig out my phone. Sookie will welcome my support now the plan is underway; she'll need it. Rapidly I check through her feed, to see if I've missed anything. She's been keeping a low profile recently. There isn't much after the summer flurry of cypress avenues and Aperol Spritzes, the bare minimum, just enough not to cause people concern. She posted yesterday but it was only an inspirational quote from Michelle Obama: *Your story is what you have, what you will always have. It is something to own.*

I send her a brief message – *Heyyyyy, been thinking about*

you, let's catch up – and my phone rings almost immediately, before I reach the bus stop. But it isn't Sookie; it's Francis. I can guess what he's after, and I can't be bothered with that at the moment. I wait until I'm on the bus to listen to his voicemail.

He's on the bike, his voice coming and going as he contends with roadworks and busy intersections. Quick question. Not about Mono, but about the music teacher. Is he right in thinking Ian Waxham was on staff in my day? Because the picture desk says Waxham has moved into Mono's Clerkenwell apartment while his protégé is away on tour (and being photographed with his girlfriend, the famous American singer-songwriter, wandering around Père Lachaise cemetery).

There's the beep of a pelican crossing, the squeak of cycle brakes. Francis puts his feet down. Yeah, so the online team are very keen on this story and Ian Waxham seems to be a great way of pulling together all the various strands: the Robbie Shepherd angle, Piper Haste *and* the Education Secretary's death spiral. The story has everything! Boarding-school abuse, Glyndebourne, the Pyramid Stage plus a political firestorm. The point is, he's wondering if I have any intel on Waxham, or if I know anyone who might.

The lights change and, pushing off, he says, 'So give me a call. Oh, and Gretchen sends her love. She's hatching a plan to get you over for supper.'

What a grotty way to make a living, I think, smartly deleting the voicemail. I can imagine an evening with Francis and Gretchen, but not how this might constitute some kind of treat for me. An odds-and-sods pity party, 'poor Ruth' chucked in with a job-lot of randoms: cousins visiting from overseas, an elderly neighbour with opinions on Meghan Markle. Chicken-thigh traybake with a couple of salad pillows, followed by an emergency pudding from the freezer section. No, thanks.

Sookie's response arrives as I get home. She has a spare ticket for the ballet and suggests we grab an early supper first. *Can't wait to see you*, she says. *Lots going on.*

* * *

The reservation is at a brasserie off St Martin's Lane. In the pre-show rush the room is warm and full of clatter, everyone – families up in town for the day, teenagers dining awkwardly with grandparents – packed elbow to elbow. I am shown to a dim corner at the back, near the kitchen doors. When Sookie is delivered to the table a few minutes later, she glances doubtfully at the chair the waiter pulls out for her. 'Isn't there anywhere else?' she asks, and somehow we end up in the window at a table for four, late sunshine sparkling on the glassware.

She's so glad I was free! She booked *Giselle* impulsively, thinking she'd take Ava, but that went down like a bucket of sick. Ava had plans to go to a party or a comedy gig – the story was not consistent – and Sookie knew better than to ask too many questions.

I wince encouragingly, and she says, 'To be fair, Ava's calmed down a bit; she's making more of an effort with me, not flying off the handle all the time. She's very excited about the new house. I can't tell you: such a relief. Once the decision was made everything just fell into place – it feels absolutely right, you know? It's like it was meant to be.'

'Wow, this is big news,' I say, and she starts to describe it to me, the new house in Brook Green and all the things that need doing to it. It's not exactly a fixer-upper, no – more of a do-over. The place was recently and expensively renovated, and that's all going into a skip: statement chandeliers, black marble bathrooms, modern parquet. The thought of all this destruction fills her with excitement. She can't wait to swing that wrecking ball.

The more she talks, the uneasier I feel, but still, when she says, 'Of course Murray would be perfectly happy to keep it exactly as it is,' I am thankful for the waiter, whose arrival with our plates creates a disturbance, allowing me to compose myself as I shake out my napkin.

He refills our glasses and moves away, and the bubble of intimacy seals us in again.

'Wait, wait – so you and Murray are back on track?' I ask, and she says, 'Oh, goodness, sorry – so much has happened since I last saw you.'

She spent the summer 'working a few things out'. On holiday she and Murray rested and swam and looked at paintings and ate delicious food, and it was, she found, a pleasure to spend time with him away from the confines of the mews house – even (for ten days or so) away from the kids, who were invited elsewhere. They managed, finally, to catch up with each other. Those warm and indolent weeks in Italy chased away her doubts, confirmed the problem had been geographical. Just as this penny was dropping, an important client requested Murray's services with a UK project, so he's back in London for the foreseeable.

Everything came together fast after that. She found the house, they made an offer, the offer was accepted, and now the contents of the Singapore apartment are being boxed up and sent home. It's all good! Well, apart from the 'Authentic Self' podcast falling through. After sitting on the proposal for ages, Jess eventually stopped replying to Sookie's emails and messages – completely unprofessional. So, when they bumped into each other at Pisa airport, Sookie didn't hold back. She had things to say, and she said them, and it felt pretty fucking great. Murray won't let her give up on the podcast idea, he thinks it's terrific. And he knows some people. Jess's loss, frankly.

The point is, as a couple they're solid. They always have been. Alone in the depressing little cottage behind Baker Street, she'd allowed herself to forget how good they were for each other. She got stuck on the Bottega Veneta bags and in doing so lost sight of what really matters. They want the same thing, they understand each other. He still does it for her. She doesn't get that from anyone else. She can't lie, it's a tremendous relief.

Unfortunately, over the summer while she was coming to her senses, Ian took it upon himself to leave his wife. This came as a shock to Sookie; yes, he'd said things from time to time, in the heat of the moment, but she had no idea he was actually going to end his marriage. If she'd known it was a possibility, she certainly wouldn't have given him any encouragement. Apparently, there was an awful scene with Carla, and the neighbours ended up calling the police; but that's on him. Nothing to do with Sookie, thank God: 'You know, he's a grown-up. He can make his own decisions. It's his life.'

Waxham's unexpected celebrity has come at a useful moment. Kayden, Mono, whatever he's called, is going above and beyond. Bigging Ian up on *Newsnight* is one thing but offering him a place to crash is quite another.

It's funny, really, because there were moments during the holidays when she managed to forget all about 'the mess with Ian' – moments when she was truly present and thankful, eating a ripe peach in the sunshine, or lying by the pool – and then Mono was suddenly blasting out at top vol, the kids having hijacked the Bluetooth. Sound of the summer, no fucking escape. Sookie sighs and forks up some frisée. She's wearing a black silk top and it's a very specific brand-new inky black, a colour quite unrelated to the black of my dress.

Carla knows her husband has been having an affair, but she doesn't know who with, and Ian has promised he won't tell. That's critical because the thing was a mistake and has run its course and Murray must never, ever get a whiff of it. The terrible revelation of his father's infidelity ended Murray's childhood, and that betrayal, the survival of it, continues to shape his expectations of himself as a husband and father. Sookie is confident Ian won't 'do anything silly' because their backstory, though completely innocent, might look compromising in a certain light. People would be quick to dust off those ancient rumours, and no one needs to be reminded that for several years Ian was Groper Chope's deputy. Ian might withstand all that rubbish if he and Sookie had a future, but not alone. Howard is all he has left now.

He still messages her several times a day, begging her to reconsider. If she's completely honest, she'd like to block him, but she can't afford to inflame the situation so she checks in regularly. She feels sorry for him, she supposes.

She puts her index finger to her touchscreen and then holds the phone for me to see.

I can't do this without you, tell me what you want, I'll do anything anything

Whatever. The end of Ian's marriage is not her concern.

It was always going to happen; probably he'd been waiting for an excuse to leave for years. Thank God she got out in time. She can hardly believe how close she came to the precipice. The children, Murray, their friends, her parents, Murray's mother – so many people would have been affected by her mistake. It amazes her, now, that she ever took Ian seriously. What possessed her? There is something in her expression, something vaguely accusatory, as if she thinks I might have played a part in this. 'You did say the sex was incredible...' I murmur, and somehow it feels a little as if I'm defensive and pushing back.

She pops a cherry tomato in her mouth. 'I may have laid that on a bit thick. Some performance issues, if I'm completely honest. Do you know, Ruth, when I look back, I think I was trying to convince you as much as myself.'

'Well, what a relief you've worked things out with Murray, such good news,' I say, 'but I guess I'm a tiny bit confused because over the summer you seemed kind of... ambivalent? I mean, you really seemed to have doubts about your marriage. I didn't imagine that, did I?'

'Oh, for sure, I may have given that impression,' she says. 'But I think maybe you read too much into it.'

I put my napkin to my mouth while she says, 'Because I had this sense – and I get it, Ruth, it's totally understandable – I had this sense that you were maybe kind of invested in a certain outcome – because of your own situation, I mean?' and though her voice goes up, as if she's uncertain and trying out a theory, that isn't what's happening here. No. She's making a point. Putting me in my place.

'But probably I got the wrong end of the stick,' she adds graciously, and then she pushes up her sleeve – that deep rich black against her skin, with its Italian tan – so she can check her watch, and signals for the bill because it's time.

Good seats in the dress circle, so you can appreciate the footwork as well as the formations of the corps de ballet. Her parents were always fussy about these things and it rubbed off on her. She passes me the programme. Flicking through the story of the peasant girl and the duke and the duke's betrothed, I become aware of her shifting position, angling her head, fiddling with her hair. When I glance sideways, her face is set in a rictus of vivid composure: half-smile, narrowed eyes blazing. It's an expression that isn't meant for me but for the thing she's holding out at arm's length, a little above eye-level, so the great curtain will appear in the background, with its monstrous festoons and tassels.

She's not at all embarrassed that I'm watching. It makes no odds to her. She maintains the pose for a moment and then she says, 'Let's get one of us together.'

She tilts her head against mine. I hate it, but I can't help it: I like it too. I am flattered that she wants to include me. I hold still and smile. Of course I'll suffer by comparison; I know my mouth won't do the right thing, my nose will be shiny, my hair will look dull and stiff. But this picture counts for something. It proves I've been admitted to the place where Sookie lives all her best lives, where she performs for the world as the person she wishes to be. It means I matter.

If Sookie can see me, so can everyone else. *Here I am*, I think. *Here I am.*

'One more for luck!' she says, and then it's done and she pulls away, her face wiped blank as an Etch-A-Sketch. Busily, she makes her selection, composes a caption. Posts.

The lamps along the balconies and boxes begin to extinguish themselves and applause breaks out as the conductor makes his way through the pit. Sookie clicks her phone into silent mode and drops it into her bag. Around us, the audience settles into the darkness like roosting birds.

The last time I saw this ballet was eight or nine years ago: my birthday, seats much higher and further back. Not really Robin's bag. It occurs to me that I haven't thought about Robin for a while, and this realisation – that I'd managed to forget his existence – shocks me, and fills me with glee.

Cottages in a clearing, peasants, a duke in disguise, love, betrayal, madness, death. Last time I took the duke's sincerity at face value and pitied him as another victim of the tragedy. That seems extraordinary to me now because Albrecht is plainly a liar, a cheat, a predatory creep who in no way deserves Giselle's final act of grace. How could I have missed that?

The spectacle plays out, and below it the rows of bows bob like components of some great industrial mechanism. In a quiet moment, as the page-turns flash, a lurch of the customary dread: can I be sure I turned it off? Now this worry displaces everything else. I imagine a notification pinging in (breaking news, or a special offer from Uber) and the tremor of horror radiating through the circle. The bone-deep shame of being that person: so careless, so selfish.

The phone is off. I always check, and then I check again. I have a clear memory of the screen going black. But you either worry about these things or you don't. I change position, but Sookie's elbow is already there on the armrest.

Gradually, the internal roar of panic fades and I can hear the music again. The lovers dance, the villagers make merry, and the hunting party arrives. Now Giselle is beginning to grasp the extent of Albrecht's deceit. She is tearing her hair loose and pulling petals from an imaginary flower. I find I have no appetite for her grief, her suffering, her madness. I will endure it in the expectation of the second act, and the cold rage of the Wilis.

When the curtain falls for the interval Sookie wants a drink. I follow her along the row, murmuring apologies, and up the stairs. There's already quite a crowd around the bar, but she has no difficulty getting served, to the indignation of the people in front of us. 'Let me get this,' I say, just as I did at the restaurant, and I offer my card as the barman pushes her G & T and my soda water over the counter, because that's how you behave when you're with her, out of politeness, or an unthinking desire to please. You end up offering things you can't really afford.

'Bit stingy with the ice,' she complains, as we carry our drinks to a corner. 'But such is life.'

'It isn't though, is it?' I say, lightly. 'Not for you,' and she puts down her drink, letting my comment settle, considering it, and then she says, 'You're quite right, Ruth, that wath a thilly thing to thay.'

She runs through her catechism, all the things for which she is grateful, counting them off on her fingers. Murray, her rock, still making her laugh, still bringing her cups of tea in bed in the morning. The kids, who are basically thriving and happy, working it all out in their own crazy way. Murray's new job. The house. So much good fortune. 'I do, I do count my blessings, I know I'm terribly lucky.' She lowers her voice. 'And I'm ashamed to admit it, but perhaps it took the thing with Ian to make me realise what was at stake – what I stood to lose. So, here's to close escapes,' and, merrily, she clinks her glass against mine.

OTHER PEOPLE'S FUN

We return to our seats with a little time to spare. Sookie is describing some charming bathroom tiles she found in Lucca that are being shipped over at great expense when her name is called. A woman is standing in the aisle, squealing and waving. 'Oh my God,' Sookie says, 'it's Amber Urquhart, I haven't seen her since Hong Kong,' and she begins to make her way back along the seats, people standing up yet again to let her pass.

Left alone, I turn on my phone. Instagram takes me straight to her post: fish gape, 'S' pendant bright against the black top, the precise comets of her eyebrows. I hadn't noticed her make-up in the restaurant or at the bar but, zooming in, I see that's the point. Behind her, the gleaming curtain, the line of lamps tapering off into the curve of the auditorium.

Sookie's post has been liked more than a hundred times, and scores of friends and strangers have felt compelled to comment. *Enjoy!* they say, and, *Looking good!* and for speed and efficiency some people simply post hearts and flames and the blowing-kisses face.

Of course she didn't put up the picture of us together. She didn't even tag me.

I glance along the row. Her back is turned. She and Amber Urquhart are deep in their reunion, laughing, marvelling at the happy absurdity of meeting like this. They're blocking the aisle steps, and people returning from the bars and the cloakrooms are wearing tight, irritated smiles as they squeeze past, but Sookie and her friend are quite oblivious. They neither notice nor care.

I shall do it.

Distantly a bell is ringing; two minutes to curtain up.

Her bag lies open at my feet, and I can see into it, I

can see the tube of hand cream with sea nutrients, and the NARS lipstick, and the tin of Swedish breath mints, and I can also see her phone, which is not turned off but is manually set to silent. I bend down and do what needs to be done and then I take the phone out of her bag and tuck it under her seat, in the gap between the tier rise and her folded jacket. Then I get to my feet, nudging her bag back into position with my shoe, and make my way along the row, again murmuring *so sorry, excuse me*, and when I reach Sookie I touch her arm and say, 'I just realised I left my card at the bar—' and she steps sideways to let me pass, busy with her friend.

I begin the ascent, pushing against the current of people returning to their seats, and at the top I go through the doorway and along a corridor, past the emptying bar and a girl collecting glasses, and the light changes, the acoustic, and I am alone on the staircase that sweeps down into the foyer, and the foyer is deserted because the bell is ringing a final warning and the second act is about to begin.

The street has been rinsed by a shower and the crowds have vanished into restaurants and theatres. The only people around are straggling parties of tourists inspecting the menus pinned up in steakhouse windows. I cross over and walk down a side street, and my mind is on a grave in a dark forest, a faraway bell tolling midnight, wraiths slipping between the trees.

Outside a noodle shop I find his number and wait for him to answer. A tuk-tuk festooned with fairy lights and plastic flowers rattles past, Lizzo on the speakers singing about tossing her hair and feeling terrific.

I apologise for calling so late, but if he's still interested I have some information on Ian Waxham.

'I'm still interested,' Francis says, and I catch the scrape of a chair leg as he stands up. I picture him miming an apology to Gretchen, rolling his eyes as he leaves the room: *work bollocks.*

There's a click as he shuts a door, and then he says, 'You know he got an honourable mention in PMQs this week?'

I heard that and saw the interview on *Channel 4 News* and read the *Times* editorial. That's really why I'm ringing. All the Waxham hagiography is causing a little disquiet. Because, you know, there are stories.

'There usually are,' he says, and waits.

'You will keep my name out of it?' I ask, and he says of course, goes without saying. He would never reveal a source.

I start by explaining why Waxham is living at Mono's flat. His wife recently threw him out. It got pretty messy and neighbours called the police. Francis makes polite noises, but I can tell he's wondering if this pathetic morsel justifies a phone call at 9 p.m.

'OK,' I say. 'There's more. The Waxhams are breaking up because he's involved with an ex-pupil. No, she isn't a recent leaver, no, she's the same vintage as me; a friend, in fact. No, hold on, I know – I'm getting to that. What I'm trying to say is, there was gossip and speculation about them years ago, when we were at Howard, at the time when Groper Chope – Waxham's head of department – was systematically abusing Robbie Shepherd and all those other little boys. It's started to dawn on us. Maybe Chope wasn't a one-off.'

When he asks if any of us reported concerns at the time, to another teacher or a parent, I say not as far as I know. Waxham had 'followers' and everyone on staff knew it, but the adults weren't particularly exercised by this stuff back then. Well, you know how it was: newspapers and films and that song by the Police normalised it, romanticised it. Teacher–pupil relationships could be star-crossed, thrilling, kind of hot – just as domestic homicides were called 'crimes of passion'. And Waxham had form. I mean, he met his wife in his first teaching post, when she was fifteen.

The point is, Waxham is still at Howard in a leadership role with responsibilities for safeguarding, and now he's being feted by celebrities and policymakers, a regular guest on daytime TV sofas and *The Moral Maze*. I tell Francis all this is particularly disturbing because he's exerted a powerful hold on my friend since she was a teenager, and now all aspects of her life are about to unravel: her marriage, her family, her mental health. She's a damaged person, though she would never admit to it: behind the impressive shopfront, she's isolated and vulnerable, easily manipulated. She's trying to end the relationship but Waxham simply won't leave her alone, he's bombarding her with messages, and his persistence could be construed as controlling and coercive.

I say I'm haunted by a photograph of them together at some school event a year ago: it's up on the Howard website, for heaven's sake.

'Is it now,' he mutters, and I can hear him tapping away, trying to find it. I'm pleased he's paying attention. After the exchange at the dispatch box, he should be able to stand this up in terms of public interest. Even if the story only starts off on page eleven or twelve and does not name her and they pixelate her face, it'll get the ball rolling. I imagine all the WhatsApp groups going batshit.

I know they've been spotted together, I say, thinking of Dribbler at the National Theatre. And if Francis wants to verify the historical aspect, he could approach Jess Carmichael, the wellness entrepreneur. There was an episode at Howard when my friend and Waxham attracted, shall we say, a *lot* of speculation, and when Jess Carmichael asked her about it at the time she was told that yes, Waxham had made a move – taken advantage, acted inappropriately, abused his position, whatever you like to call it.

Jess might be responsive because she and my friend recently had a nasty falling-out. Scenes in the departure lounge at Pisa airport. God only knows. As an afterthought, I mention Jess is launching a Skyros retreat designed to address the allostatic load (intention ceremonies, gong baths, gut-enrichment programmes) and will be keen for coverage. He says he'll have a chat with other sections before he makes the call.

I say it's definitely worth trying Carla, Waxham's wife. She may have things to say at this point.

There's a pause, and during it I hear the beep of an incoming call, someone trying to contact me. 'So go on, let's have it,' he says. 'Who is she, this friend of yours?'

'You won't name her, will you?'

No, he says, reassuringly, and then he tells me what I already know: she has certain rights as a victim; no media outlet will compromise her privacy. He doesn't say there will be a free-for-all on social media, and one of the *Carmina Burana* sopranos (parked up, bored, waiting for a child to come out of maths tutoring) will post Sookie's name on Facebook, and by the end of the day everyone who matters will know. And though she will swear it's over and Waxham meant nothing to her, Murray will not believe her, because it turns out she's been lying to him for months and months – maybe much longer. No one can be sure.

'Who is she?' Francis repeats.

This is it: the point when I let go and trust to fate. It's a moment of excitement and possibility, and I am enjoying it, but I mustn't draw it out any longer because the second act is underway, and in the dark forest Myrtha, Queen of the Wilis, is summoning her spectral battalion who will shortly dance Hilarion to death. So I come straight out with it: *it's Sookie Inchcape, Murray's wife.*

The keyboard clicks stop for a moment and I can hear his breath as he takes stock. 'OK, can't say I was expecting that,' he says. 'She certainly made an impression when we met. Very... *self-assured*,' and I guess this means she didn't defer to or flirt with him; she didn't bother to court his approval. She didn't need to. Maybe he longed, even then, to take her down a peg or two. And Murray – who is, after all, so extraordinarily successful.

'Of course,' he adds thoughtfully, 'Sookie must be finding all this media posturing pretty, um, *triggering*. I wonder if she'll talk.'

'She might, if you catch her at the right moment,' I say. 'For instance, I know she's on her own this evening – you could try her now.' I tell him not to worry if she doesn't answer immediately. No point in leaving a message. Just press redial. Keep trying. She'll pick up in the end. She always does.

I send him her number and then there's the tiresome fussy business of ending the conversation, navigating his thanks and ludicrous assurances that the story is in the best possible hands. He's just as keen to get rid of me: he's going to make the call straightaway, as soon as we hang up. 'Great, goodbye,' I say, and then I press the red button.

There's a voicemail waiting for me, a notification from

the missed call. I stand in front of the noodle shop, listening to the message as a waiter places a bowl in front of a solitary diner who is seated in the window. Nell's voice, tired and excited, almost anxious. She just landed at Heathrow and is waiting for her luggage. Is everything OK? Because she's had the weirdest feeling recently. She can't really explain it but anyway – she missed me, she had a longing to see me, so she booked a flight. She wants to catch up, hang out – all the things you can't do properly over WhatsApp or FaceTime, even if you have a signal. She wonders when I'm free.

The diner unwraps his chopsticks and the steam twists up towards the pendant bulb, clouding the window.

At this moment the moon will be rising over the forest, casting its cold light upon the glade where Myrtha is gathering her attendants. The Wilis will arrange their arms and turn their shrouded faces away, drifting over the stage like mist, and the hush will be so deep that the people in the front rows will hear the soft blunt flutter of the bourrées. Necks, shoulders, wrists, hands: what a relief, to leave the world behind, escaping to a place where everything is so quiet and beautiful, where the wildest and ugliest of feelings are disciplined and turned into something exquisite.

It's almost unbearable, to think of that sound breaking out: the handclaps, beeps and bumps, the jump-rope chant which is also a call to arms. There is a chance Sookie will stoop and grope for her bag as soon as she hears the opening notes, but, knowing her, I think it's far more likely she'll perform a swift calculation and – while the people around her shift indignantly in their seats, trying to divine the source of the sound – she'll sit tight, waiting for the voicemail to kick in, her eyes innocently fixed on the stage.

On and on it goes at top volume, that fierce beat hissing and sparking around the dark auditorium like a loose electrical cable. Four seconds. Five. Six. Seven. Each an eternity. Outrage will chase along the rows, sweeping through the circle and the stalls and into the boxes. It will reach up into the gods and down into the orchestra pit. On stage, every last dancer in those precise ghostly formations will feel it, and they will all hate her for it. They may not know who she is but they will know the sort of person she is, and they will never forgive her.

The ringtone will shut off abruptly, and she will think: *it's over. I got away with it.* Then it will start again, and it will never really stop, not for her. It's only just beginning, as far as she's concerned.

In the noodle shop window, the solitary diner is busy with his bowl, his features blurred by the steam on the glass. I turn away and walk on, towards the bright coloured lights, and as I approach the station the clamour of the city gathers around me, the traffic and the music and the conversations, the stories that people tell each other about themselves. It's all there, and I can take it or leave it. It's up to me. *Here I am*, I think. *Here I am.*

Acknowledgements

With love and thanks to:

Poppy and Barnaby Critchlow

Sara and David Lane

The FWC: Helen Papaleontiou and Rachael Tiffen. Also Georgia and Ines Aberdeen, and Clemency and Ethan Tiffen

Amanda Coe, Morag Preston, Jane Dwelly, Becky Morris, Peggy Vance, Daisy Cook, Olivia Lacey, Lucy Darwin, Alison Critchlow, Lynne Riley, Damian Whitworth, Andrew Clifford, Rachel Thomas, Annalisa D'Innella, Megan Carver, Kasia Czernia, Liz Dormandy, Fiona Walker, Jo White, Vicky Nichols, Grace Farrugia, Olivia Bell

Lucia Gahlin, who showed me the Petrie Museum shabtis

My agent, Karolina Sutton

My editor, Juliet Annan, and all at Weidenfeld & Nicolson, particularly Sarah Fortune; as well as Gráinne Fox, Helen O'Hare, and the team at Little, Brown and Company

Always missing Susie Steiner and Deb Dooley